Kate Fortu

You don't get to be my age without recognizing when the wool is being pulled over someone's eyes! And I suspect my dear Tyler is holding something back from the Fortune family. Now, I know Tyler's parents gave him a silly marriage ultimatum and I've never met any of his women friends before, but something tells me that he barely knows his bride-to-be. As the family matriarch, I could put an end to this marriage nonsense. But Julie Parker is the best thing to happen to Tyler.

And some well-intentioned meddling by a harmless old woman may be just what the doctor ordered. I'm going to plan their wedding, help Julie find a wedding gown and take her for a makeover.... And when I'm done, Julie, Tyler is going to be dazzled speechless!

Dear Reader,

As we celebrate Silhouette's 20th anniversary year as a romance publisher, we invite you to welcome in the fall season with our latest six powerful, passionate, provocative love stories from Silhouette Desire!

In September's MAN OF THE MONTH, fabulous Peggy Moreland offers a *Slow Waltz Across Texas*. In order to win his wife back, a rugged Texas cowboy must learn to let love into his heart. Popular author Jennifer Greene delivers a special treat for you with *Rock Solid,* which is part of the highly sensual Desire promotion, BODY & SOUL.

Maureen Child's exciting miniseries, BACHELOR BATTALION, continues with *The Next Santini Bride,* a responsible single mom who cuts loose with a handsome Marine. The next installment of the provocative Desire miniseries FORTUNE'S CHILDREN: THE GROOMS is *Mail-Order Cinderella* by Kathryn Jensen, in which a plain-Jane librarian seeks a husband through a matchmaking service and winds up with a Fortune! Ryanne Corey returns to Desire with a *Lady with a Past,* whose true love woos her with a chocolate picnic. And a nurse loses her virginity to a doctor in a night of passion, only to find out the next day that her lover is her new boss, in *Doctor for Keeps* by Kristi Gold.

Be sure to indulge yourself this autumn by reading all six of these tantalizing titles from Silhouette Desire!

Enjoy!

Joan Marlow Golan

Joan Marlow Golan
Senior Editor, Silhouette Desire

Please address questions and book requests to:
Silhouette Reader Service
U.S.: 3010 Walden Ave., P.O. Box 1325, Buffalo, NY 14269
Canadian: P.O. Box 609, Fort Erie, Ont. L2A 5X3

Mail-Order Cinderella

KATHRYN JENSEN

Silhouette®

Desire

Published by Silhouette Books

America's Publisher of Contemporary Romance

If you purchased this book without a cover you should be aware that this book is stolen property. It was reported as "unsold and destroyed" to the publisher, and neither the author nor the publisher has received any payment for this "stripped book."

Special thanks and acknowledgment are given to
Kathryn Jensen for her contribution to
Fortune's Children: The Grooms series.

To Janet Tanke, the editor I'm so sadly losing, for overseeing the creation of this novel, lovingly and with professional dedication from beginning to finish. And to Ann Leslie Tuttle, the editor I'm happily gaining, who has already taken on the mantles of muse, cheerleader and creative partner. Without such enthusiasm and loyalty, an author's world would be a much bleaker place. K.J.

 SILHOUETTE BOOKS

ISBN 0-373-76318-2

MAIL-ORDER CINDERELLA

Copyright © 2000 by Harlequin Books. S.A.

All rights reserved. Except for use in any review, the reproduction or utilization of this work in whole or in part in any form by any electronic, mechanical or other means, now known or hereafter invented, including xerography, photocopying and recording, or in any information storage or retrieval system, is forbidden without the written permission of the editorial office, Silhouette Books, 300 East 42nd Street, New York, NY 10017 U.S.A.

All characters in this book have no existence outside the imagination of the author and have no relation whatsoever to anyone bearing the same name or names. They are not even distantly inspired by any individual known or unknown to the author, and all incidents are pure invention.

This edition published by arrangement with Harlequin Books S.A.

® and TM are trademarks of Harlequin Books S.A., used under license. Trademarks indicated with ® are registered in the United States Patent and Trademark Office, the Canadian Trade Marks Office and in other countries.

Visit Silhouette at www.eHarlequin.com

Printed in U.S.A.

Books by Kathryn Jensen

Silhouette Desire

I Married a Prince #1115
The Earl Takes a Bride #1282
Mail-Order Cinderella #1318

Silhouette Intimate Moments

Time and Again #685
Angel's Child #758
The Twelve-Month Marriage #797

KATHRYN JENSEN

has written many novels for young readers as well as for adults. She speed walks, works out with weights and enjoys ballroom dancing for exercise, stress reduction and pleasure. Her children are now grown. She lives in Maryland with her writing companion—Sunny, a lovable terrier-mix adopted from a shelter.

Having worked as a hospital switchboard operator, department store sales associate, bank clerk and elementary school teacher, she now splits her days between writing her own books and teaching fiction writing at two local colleges and through a correspondence course. She enjoys helping new writers get a start and speaks "at the drop of a hat" at writers' conferences, libraries and schools across the country.

F💠RTUNE'S
Children

Meet the Arizona Fortunes—a family with a legacy of wealth, influence and power. As they gather for a host of weddings, a shocking plot against the family is revealed...and passionate new romances are ignited.

TYLER FORTUNE: This sexy man-about-town knew how to drive a rivet with the best of his construction crew and kiss a woman senseless, but he didn't think he knew anything about marriage. Until plain-Jane Julie became his bride....

JULIE PARKER: All this shy librarian had wanted was a quiet, undemanding man who'd give her a baby—instead, she got a stunningly sexy, self-possessed man whose kisses gave her an unexpected glimpse of heaven.

JASON FORTUNE: Maybe if his younger brother, Tyler, had stuck with one girlfriend for more than three months, he'd know that finding a bride wasn't like ordering a pizza!

One

Tyler Fortune hated losing a fight, and today he'd lost big time. Now he was going to pay for it, and the price was...marriage.

His sole consolation was that he'd relinquish his freedom on his own terms. He'd be damned if he let his parents corral him into marrying a snooty Tucson debutante or one of their wealthy friends' daughters.

Impatiently, he shoved another videotape into the VCR. The custom-made entertainment center was built into one mahogany-paneled wall of his office on the fifth floor of the Fortune Building. Hitting the play button on the remote, he sat down again and leaned back in his chair to view the screen over the wide knuckles of his interlocked fingers.

A woman wearing more makeup than most cosmetic counters stocked beamed into the camera and introduced herself in an irritating falsetto. He groaned aloud. This wife-hunting business was hard, nerve-racking work, and probably a waste of time.

Tyler deeply resented lost minutes that were turning into hours. Hours he desperately needed to put into his family's business. Why couldn't his father, of all people, see that? Hell, by now he might have made that trip to Dallas they'd discussed, and secured another multi-million-dollar contract.

Although there was the occasional exception, Tyler rarely took time off from the work he loved. A short, intense workout at the Saguaro Springs Health Club. Dinner with a beautiful woman at Tucson's magnificent Janos— followed by a night's companionship, because he was, after all, a healthy male. Once in a while, his former college roommate, Dave Johnson, talked him into an extreme-sports adventure—skydiving over the Grand Canyon, white-water rafting in Montana, rock climbing in Colorado.

Dangerous sports duplicated the risk and thrill of balancing atop a steel girder three hundred feet above the merciless ground, or closing a hard-fought deal. Tyler's life was the company. That was how he liked it. And, dammit, if he had his way…that was how it would remain!

But his parents' persistent attempts at matchmaking had drastically increased in recent months. And Grandmother Kate had arrived from Minneapolis—the equivalent of bringing in the heavy artillery. Jasmine and Devlin's plots to marry him off would have seemed old-fashioned and ludicrous had they not been so seriously aimed at him. Earlier that day, his father had delivered an ultimatum, "You are going to marry and settle into family life by the time you turn thirty, or you won't inherit your share of the company. It's for your own good, Tyler. And for the good of this family."

Tensing again at the thought of complications a wife and family would inflict upon his well-ordered bachelor life, Tyler viciously jammed his thumb down on the eject button. Out popped the fifth videotape. He shoved in a new one, returned to his seat. Lifted rangy blue-jeaned legs to prop his boot heels on the edge of the blueprint-cluttered desk and slouched in his chair, muttering to himself. A sprinkle of dry red clay sifted over the tooled-leather desk blotter. He ignored it and tried to focus on the task at hand, protecting his position as heir to the vice presidency of Fortune Construction Company.

Tyler aimed steel-gray eyes at the woman being interviewed. There was a too-eager sparkle in her eyes. Carmine-red lipstick slashed across her full lips. A wave of blond hair swept seductively over one eye. Okay—this one was pretty. Stretching it, maybe even beautiful. She was young, energetic, quick with her answers and claimed she was willing to "have children after a while."

An alarm sounded in his subconscious. *After a while.* Female code words for *I don't want to ruin my figure until I'm too old to care.* He chuckled. Dear Kate would have a serious problem with this one. His sprightly octogenarian grandmother made no secret of the fact she wanted great-grandkids by the truckload, ASAP! Smiling and shaking his head, he hit the eject button.

"Last one of the batch. You'd better be a winner, sweetheart," Tyler muttered as he slid in the final cartridge and hit play.

"I really hope this isn't what I think it is," a low voice stated from the open doorway.

Tyler looked around with a laconic smile at his brother Jason. "I don't waste my time on *those* kinds of flicks. The real thing is so much more satisfying."

Wearing an amused grin, Jason leaned against the doorjamb, just as tall, sinewy and muscled as his younger brother, but with a touch more red in his dark hair, and amber instead of gray eyes. Nevertheless, they shared the proud heritage of their father's mother, Natasha Lightfoot, a full-blooded Papago Indian. Both brothers' features bore the brand of their Native American ancestry—sharply angled cheek bones, strong aquiline noses, jaws that might have been carved from the hard red sandstone of the sacred plateau north of town.

Jason observed the image flickering on the screen with mock solemnity. "Doesn't seem to have much of a plot."

"Not s'posed to," Tyler drawled, turning back to find a pale oval face on the TV screen. He stared, surprised by what he saw. This one was...different.

The young woman spoke quietly, almost as if afraid someone might hear her. She wasn't trying to sell herself or flirt with the camera as the others had before her. She appeared not to have worn any makeup at all, but the harsh studio lights might have washed out a light application. No jewelry of any kind was evident at her throat, earlobes, or wrists. If one word described her, it was *plain*.

Nevertheless, something about the woman pulled at Tyler, held his gaze, captured his attention just as strongly as the others hadn't.

Jason scowled. "Is this a new technique for interviewing receptionists?"

"Brides."

His brother's sudden laughter rocked the room. "Yeah, right." Jason gasped to catch his breath and wiped at his eyes. "Brides."

"I'm serious. If I have to marry in less than a year, I'll be damned if I'm going to let anyone pick out a wife for me."

"Do you really think Dad's serious about this?" Jason asked.

"He made clear just how serious over lunch today. Luckily, I had a backup plan ready."

Jason shook his head. "This isn't a backup plan—it's a disaster. You can't find a wife this way, Ty!"

"Why not?" Tyler demanded stubbornly. He resented anyone telling him how he should live his life, and he made no exception for his brother or cousins, all of whom helped in the family business. "Who makes the rules for wife-choosing? Hell, they wanted you to marry Cara when you got her pregnant, back when you were only twenty years old! I don't want to end up like—"

Too late, he stopped himself. The final word, *you,* hung as a silent rebuke in the air between them. He wished he'd kept his mouth shut. He hadn't meant to sound so critical, or remind Jason of his ill-fated first marriage.

"Sorry, I didn't mean—"

Jason waved off his apology.

"Look, I tried to tell Dad I'm not cut out for marriage, but he won't listen. And I just don't have time to do this any other way."

There were many things Tyler felt capable of handling well. He knew how to set a half-ton I-beam ten floors above the desert, how to pour a foundation that wouldn't crack even in the unforgiving Arizona heat, how to drive a rivet with the best of his crew and how to kiss a woman crazy. But marriage?

Jason seemed less interested in his sibling's explanations than he was in the petite, nervous creature on the wide-screen TV. "Look at her. You'd think the interviewer was a lion about to devour her."

"She does look about to jump out of her skin," Tyler admitted. Her eyes were huge and blinked, blinked,

blinked...like those of a wild animal startled by headlights. She repeatedly moistened her lips with the tip of her tongue. For once the gesture didn't look contrived or seductive. Nevertheless, Tyler found it appealing, innocently tantalizing. He'd have settled for seeing her jump out of her clothes.

Jason sighed. "I don't understand why people put themselves through this sort of meat-market inspection. It's as bad as hanging out in a singles bar."

"Who knows. Loneliness? A desire to be part of something? A couple...a family."

But Tyler already had a family—all he'd ever wanted anyway. His brother, niece, parents, grandmother and cousins formed one rowdy, hardworking, competitive, proud clan. He loved them all fiercely. He wasn't interested in bringing an intruder into their midst, and he didn't see why his parents had become so insistent that he should.

Amazingly, he still couldn't take his eyes from the timid woman's face. "Julie," he heard the off-screen interviewer ask her, "why did you apply to Soulmate Search?"

She straightened her spine, hitched back her narrow shoulders and lifted her chin to look directly into the camera for the first time. Tyler was certain the effort to make the simple postural adjustments was enormous.

"I want a baby," she said crisply.

"Oh boy, kiss of death," Jason muttered.

Tyler slowly shook his head. Someone ought to tell her honesty wouldn't get her very far in the dating world. She was just making herself sound needy. Needy didn't turn guys on.

"You mean," the interviewer suggested, trying to steer her toward a more appealing reply, "you'd like to find your soul mate, someone to share your interests like gourmet cooking and love of children?"

"No," Julie said slowly, emphasizing each subsequent word as if it contained a message of its own, "all... I...want...is...a...child. Children actually. Three, four... more if my husband wants them. I adore children."

Tyler wondered if therein lay a hidden meaning. Children were great, but she wasn't too crazy about grown men?

"I see," mumbled the interviewer. In the background, pages were being noisily shuffled. She'd put him off his rhythm.

Julie...what was her last name? Tyler glanced at the letter that had accompanied the tapes. Parker. Yes, Julie Ann Parker was just too earnest for this sophisticated matchmaking service with its nationwide offices.

Tyler felt embarrassed for her. He pushed the eject button on the remote. The tape smoothly slid out of the VCR.

"Nice girl," Jason commented. "Doesn't have a clue, does she?"

"Huh? Oh, no..." Tyler was still thinking about Julie Parker's eyes. He couldn't remember their color—hazel, he thought. A subtle hue not terribly distinctive or memorable. But they displayed a nebulous quality he would very much like to explore in person. And that flick of soft pink tongue every now and then...lordy, what that did to his lower regions.

Maybe he should run the tape again. Just for the heck of it.

"Well, good luck, Romeo," Jason said cheerfully. "Personally, I think if you stuck with one girlfriend for more than three months, you might find one with long-term potential."

"It's not *their* staying power I worry about."

Man to man—the universal question. Will one woman ever be enough for me...for the rest of my life?

"Yeah, well." Jason shrugged. "You never know until the right one comes along. When she's meant for you, everything falls into place. Look at how Adele has changed my view of marriage." He broke out in a boyish grin that Tyler envied. What he wouldn't give to feel that carefree in the middle of all they had been going through in recent weeks.

Tyler changed the subject. "So, what brought you down here this late in the day?" His brother was VP in charge of marketing, and had relatively little to do with the construction end of the business.

Jason's smile slid away as he moved farther inside his brother's office and closed the door behind him. "Something you ought to know about before the press catches wind. Link Templeton thinks he's found evidence that Mike Dodd was...well, that elevator he was on might not have crashed fifteen floors without a little help."

Only a few weeks ago, a fatal accident at the building site of the Fortune Memorial Children's Hospital had taken the life of their foreman. When the police didn't immediately declare Dodd's death accidental, the Fortunes called in a private investigator to help get to the bottom of the incident quickly and reassure investors.

Tyler dropped his boot heels from the desktop with a thud and shot to his feet. "Are you sure? Is *he* sure?"

"Link's a pretty cautious guy. He wouldn't come out with some outrageous theory unless he had proof. He believes the elevator was sabotaged, which means Mike might have been intentionally killed."

"You mean murdered." Now that it had been said out loud, Tyler felt it must be true.

Dodd had been a crucial cog in the hospital project, which was a labor of love for the Fortunes. Everyone in the family was taking part—raising money, putting in unpaid hours of labor, donating materials, gathering regional and state political support and local sympathy for a medical facility that would serve the young, ethnically diverse population around Pueblo.

Once the hospital was complete, injured and sick children wouldn't need to be rushed off to Tucson, twenty-five miles to the north, for medical care. Papago families would receive care for their children without requiring proof of insurance or demands that they pay astronomical medical costs they couldn't afford. This had been his family's dream for as long as Tyler had been in the business, and that was as far back as he could remember.

If someone wanted to hurt the Fortunes, sabotaging the hospital was a perfect way to do it.

"This is terrible. Have you told Dad yet?"

Jason lifted a hand in a helpless gesture. "I'm on my way to the ranch right now."

Tyler nodded grimly. A family didn't acquire the wealth of the Fortunes without making enemies along the way. But he hadn't wanted to believe envy and greed could push anyone in Pueblo to murder.

"You want to come with me when I give Dad the news?" Jason asked.

Tyler found himself staring at the dark TV screen. "No. You go ahead, I'll get the details later. Too much to do here."

Jason shook his head as if he understood the flow of his brother's thoughts. "You can't order a wife as if she were a pizza."

Tyler flicked a piece of lint off his denim shirt. "Marriages used to be arranged on a lot less than a videotape."

"You're crazy, you know that?" Jason threw his strong arms around Tyler and thumped him fondly on the back.

Minutes later, Tyler found himself standing in the middle of his office, still staring at the dark TV screen. Was he crazy for wanting to take command of his own future? Women made demands on their men. Children required unlimited love and constant attention to their physical needs. All of that time spent relating to family members ate up precious work hours and changed a man. Whether he wanted to be changed or not.

The cold, black expanse of screen challenged Tyler. Alternatives. He desperately needed alternatives. Tyler reached for the remote again. Julie Parker's smooth, pale countenance materialized before him.

He was partial to flaming redheads. Miss Parker's hair was paper-bag brown. He melted in the presence of blue eyes. Hers were a subtle mossy hue. Tall, leggy women instantly attracted him. He glanced down at the stats accompanying her tape. She was barely five-foot-two. He'd tower over her.

She was all wrong for him physically. But he could tell by her shy manner, frequent blushes, and the way she repeatedly averted her eyes from the camera that she wasn't the type to assert herself. *This might actually work to your advantage,* a persistent voice whispered to him. And all she asked from him was a baby.

She needed a husband; he needed a wife. A simple trade-off.

She had just about given up hope. In less than ten days, the six-month membership Julie had purchased in the upscale matchmaking service would expire. She couldn't afford to sign up for another. She could barely afford next month's rent.

That same night, the telephone rang. "We've received a request for a personal contact," the woman on the other end cheerfully informed her. "I can overnight a copy of the gentleman's tape to you. Let us know if you'd like to meet him. He looks like an excellent match for you, Miss Parker.''

Julie was skeptical. Her first thought was: This is the bait to make me sign up for another six months.

But when the tape arrived along with a brief biographical sketch, she wondered if this might actually be the moment she'd been waiting for. Someone was interested in meeting her! And he knew from the start what she looked like, how awkwardly she behaved around strangers and what she expected of him.

Last fall, it had taken every ounce of her precious store of courage to contact Soulmate Search after rejecting every other dating service in the phone book because they'd seemed embarrassingly tacky if not outright perilous. Imagine divulging your private hopes and dreams to hundreds of absolute strangers! And they could just forget about her climbing into a car with a stranger.

But this company guaranteed confidentiality and a thorough screening of applicants to weed out undesirables. She would receive names and video interviews of men from all across the country who were serious about marriage and potentially interested in her. Soulmate's clients were men and women with stable incomes who wouldn't mind flying to the opposite coast to meet a potential mate. No lounge lizards, prison inmates or out-of-work loafers here!

The next day Julie had blown her entire savings on one last-ditch effort to find a man who could give her what she so desperately needed.

Now her heart beat frantically in her chest and her fingertips felt moist as she slipped the tape cartridge into the used video player she'd purchased for ten dollars at the thrift shop. Julie poured herself a glass of the generic Chablis she kept handy as a cooking ingredient. The love she would have lavished on a child she put into creating exotic dishes, even though she had no one to share them with in her tiny apartment. She took three fast sips to steady her nerves, then pushed a button and stood back from the screen, her grocery-store wineglass cupped between trembling hands.

The man on the screen was drop-dead gorgeous. This had to be a mistake.

Julie ejected the film, inspected the label, reread the accompanying letter.

No, everything appeared to be in order. His name was Tyler Fortune, just as the woman on the phone had said. He lived in Pueblo, Arizona, almost due west of Houston, where she lived. This was good. She felt better knowing they both resided in the Southwest.

Julie started the tape again.

She sat down without looking to see if a chair was nearby, and her bottom made serendipitous contact with a sofa cushion. Hugging her knees to her chest, she held her breath while the amazing man on the screen answered a list of questions posed by a female interviewer.

"What line of work are you in, Mr. Fortune?" the woman asked.

"Construction."

Ah, Julie thought, so that's how he got those strong neck and shoulder muscles—swinging a pickax, hefting lumber, lugging sacks of cement mix. Even in a respectable dress shirt and tie, he clearly was a well-formed man.

"And your hobbies?"

"Not many."

"Name one or two, please."

"I, um, well, I like the outdoors."

Great! Children should play outside a lot. She wasn't

very athletic herself, so it would be wonderful if their father took them on hikes, fishing, played ball with them.

"Is marriage a high or low priority for you, Mr. Fortune?"

"Very high," he answered solemnly, his gray eyes steady and calm.

A little yelp of joy escaped Julie's lips. She took a quick sip of wine, then giggled as some dribbled down her chin. And this man had liked her tape!

"What about children?"

"Yes, there definitely need to be children in my marriage."

This was almost too good to be true! Perhaps these were the very reasons this Tyler Fortune found her tape appealing. He obviously wanted a family just as much as she did. He was a man capable of looking beyond her ordinary appearance and nervous responses, to more important and practical issues. To a future that could be good for both of them.

But there was one thing that bothered her. She'd learned to be wary of handsome men. A man who was too good-looking usually knew it and took full advantage. Tyler Fortune should have been awash with women. There must be something drastically wrong with the man.

Julie watched the interview all the way through to the end, rewound, then watched it three more times—accompanied by three more glasses of wine. Instead of defects showing up, Tyler looked better and better with each playing, and each glass of wine. He seemed to be staring straight through the camera lens at her. Only her. His gaze was direct, intelligent and sometimes playful. He was a man she at least could like, if not love. He was a man who made strange, tickley things happen inside her.

Turning off the TV, Julie picked up the letter that had

come with the tape. She rolled the side of the wineglass across her forehead, cooling her feverish skin. She thought about possibilities...dreams...a future. And risks.

The letter said it was now up to her to contact Mr. Fortune if she was interested in meeting with him. He had not been given her address or phone number, in case she decided against following up on his invitation to call.

"It's not really a date," she whispered. "It's more like a business meeting, isn't it?"

Call it what you will, this may be your last chance, a voice nagged from a fragile, worried corner of her soul.

"I know," she said. "I know."

Two

Tyler was prepared for the worst when he arrived early and parked outside Van Gogh's, just north of Westheimer. The trendy Houston restaurant was nestled on immaculately landscaped grounds. Along the sloping grass that ran down to the bayou, the famous peacocks were strutting their stuff for tourists wielding zoom-lensed cameras.

He parked within easy sight of the main entrance to the restaurant, hoping to see Julie arrive. If she looked just too dreadful to consider marrying, he'd make the meal a quick one then send flowers to her home the next day. The polite note accompanying them would thank her for her gracious company then explain that he felt they weren't as natural a match as he'd hoped.

However, as he sat restlessly in the sleek Lincoln Continental he'd rented earlier that afternoon at Hobby Airport, he doubted the remaining six months before his thirtieth birthday would bring a more suitable prospect.

He waited nervously, trying to recall her most promising traits. Julie seemed polite, moral, genuinely fond of children and interested in the domestic arts. When they'd spoken on the phone two days after Tyler had first seen Julie on her tape, she'd mentioned her love of cooking twice. He assumed she'd eventually become so busy with the children and her own interests, he wouldn't need to worry about changing his life much at all. If Julie did object to his long working hours, he'd just put her straight, and, as meek as she was, she wasn't likely to insist.

Something told him she wouldn't be terribly demanding in bed either.

Maybe it was her naturally quiet nature. Her voice over the phone that night he'd called had been as sweet and shy as on the tape. He'd started to ask about her sexual history, which seemed to him a logical question for two people considering making babies together. But she became so flustered he immediately bailed out, deciding to wait until they could discuss the subject face-to-face.

Tyler looked down at his hands and found he was gripping the Lincoln's steering wheel as tightly as if he were maneuvering through careening traffic. Deliberately, he loosened his fingers. Women never made him nervous. Why should this little mouse?

At last a faded red subcompact pulled up hesitantly in front of Van Gogh's entrance. The driver seemed confused when the valet tried to open her door for her. Tyler couldn't help smiling. After several minutes of animated conversation, the young man coaxed the woman out of her car and took her place in the driver's seat. She stood at the curb, staring after her vehicle as it disappeared around the corner, as though expecting never to see it again.

This could be none other than his Julie Parker.

Her charming naïveté tugged at Tyler's heart. He decided he couldn't in good conscience let her walk into the restaurant alone and deal with Jean Paul. The maître d's icy French scowl would be enough to send her scurrying home.

Quickly, Tyler let himself out of the car and jogged across the street, punching the button on his electronic key to lock the car doors as his long legs ate up pavement. Just as Julie's hand reached with an obvious tremor for the polished brass door handle, he caught up with her.

"Allow me," he said, stretching around her to open the door.

Julie caught her breath as if she hadn't been aware anyone was behind her. "Oh. Thank you." She blinked up at him warily, and he was struck again by the subtle variations of colors in the irises. Her breath across his nostrils was petal-sweet. "You're Mr. Fortune?"

"Tyler." Placing his free hand at the small of her back, he guided her inside. "I just arrived myself. And you're Julie, right?"

"Oh, well, yes," she managed.

"Here, let me take your coat." It was still chilly for a Texas March. The Southwest had seen an unusually cold winter. People were wearing wool coats and scarves that hadn't been taken out of closets in years.

"Thank you," she murmured again, flicking her eyes up at him for a hasty view of his face before she looked around the foyer.

It was designed to resemble a Roman grotto—bare stone, little sprigs of green growing between the rough gray rocks. A waterfall splashed sedately at the far end, near the dining rooms. He'd chosen this restaurant because it felt like his turf. Rugged yet refined. Sophisticated…quiet…intimate. He'd flown dates to Houston for a weekend when he didn't want the whole town of Pueblo gossiping about who their most eligible bachelor was seeing socially. The restaurant's atmosphere was tinged with upper-class seduction. He felt his body react mildly to the suggestion, and he folded his hands in front of himself.

"I apologize for not noticing you sooner," Julie said softly. "I was looking for Arizona plates on the cars along the street."

"I picked up a rental at the airport," he explained.

"You *flew* to Houston? Oh my, that must have cost a fortune."

"Things were pretty busy at the job site. I didn't want to—" He stopped himself before saying *waste the time.* "I didn't want to be away too long."

"I see." She smiled up at him as if impressed by his strong work ethics. "I know how that is. I hate to leave a job half done." Her eyes widened as a woman in a long black crepe gown slit up to her thigh passed them. She wore a diamond ankle bracelet. Glancing down self-consciously at her neat wool skirt and matching sweater set, Julie grimaced. "I think I may be a little underdressed for this place."

Tyler shook his head. "Not at all. You look fine."

She stared at him for a second, as though trying to determine whether he was being honest or just hoping to make her feel better. He kept his expression blank. Sighing, she changed the subject. "Your job in construction…what exactly do you do? Run heavy equipment? Hammer nails and such?"

He laughed. "Not ordinarily, although I can handle both."

Jean Paul arrived at that moment, saving him from admitting more than he chose to just yet. Tyler had intentionally skirted a full explanation of his work, as well as specifics about himself and his family. Such as the fact that the Fortunes were the wealthiest and most influential residents of southern Arizona. He'd wanted to see Julie's reaction to him as a person before he revealed that marrying him would make her a wealthy woman.

When they were seated, he ordered wine and suggested two specialties of the house. She eagerly agreed to the seafood. The sommelier presented the wine, a rare white merlot, opened the bottle, offered Tyler the cork then poured when he'd approved. At last, all the servers left them alone.

"Tell me about yourself," he said.

Julie lifted the crystal stem to her lips and sipped cautiously. "There isn't a lot to tell. Most everything was in the bio Soulmate gave you." She sipped again, and grinned like a child secretly allowed a sweet between meals.

He thought the guilty twinkle in her eyes charming. It brought out a wicked side of him that whispered how much fun it might be to shock her and set those fascinating, multicolored eyes afire. He attempted to undress her mentally, but her conservative outfit didn't give his imagination much to work with.

"Oh my, this is delicious. I sometimes treat myself to a glass of wine after work. But one bottle lasts me a month, and it never tastes this good."

She lifted her glass and took another delicate mouthful. Her eyes fluttered closed, and she tilted her head back as she swallowed. Her elegant throat taunted him, and he suddenly ached to reach across the table and smooth his open palm down the flow of ivory flesh. "We can have a different wine with our meal if you like."

Julie's eyes flew wide with alarm. "Oh, no, we mustn't. This meal is going to be expensive enough." She leaned over the table and whispered conspiratorially to him. "One thing you should know right now, Mr. Fortune—"

"Tyler."

"Tyler. One thing you should understand," she said earnestly, "is that I can't afford to marry a man who doesn't know the value of a dollar. If I stay at home with my children...our children...we'll have to live on your salary alone. A construction worker's pay these days may be adequate for a comfortable life, but it won't allow for many nights like this."

"No, I'm sure it wouldn't." He hadn't intended to lead her on. However, he still needed to know a little more about Julie before admitting how little he worried about the cost of lavish dinners for his dates.

She rested back in her chair and observed him solemnly. "I'm sorry if I've been too blunt. I believe in living within one's means...that's all."

"Perfectly understandable," he replied. "I want to know exactly what you expect of me. And I'll be very frank about what I can and can't do for you. But first I need you to tell me who Julie Parker really is. There's a lot more that goes into a person than a job and a few hobbies."

"It's not a very interesting story," she said apologetically.

"Let me be the judge." He gave her an encouraging wink that seemed to put her more at ease.

"Well, I was born in Houston, never lived more than two miles from the neighborhood where I grew up and I've traveled only as far as New Mexico in one direction, Arkansas in the other. I graduated from the University of Houston, then took a job at the southwestern branch of the public library. I've always loved books; they've been my friends since childhood. It seemed natural to want to become a librarian.''

He nodded. "So you spend every day surrounded by tomes and silence?''

"I'm never bored, if that's what you're implying,'' she said with unexpected energy. "But sometimes I do wish I could travel. After the bills are paid, there isn't much left for zipping off to Europe.'' She laughed to herself and shook her head wistfully, as if this was a fantasy normal people didn't take seriously.

Tyler had been to England and the Continent fifteen times since he graduated from college. "I expect not,'' he murmured diplomatically.

"Well,'' she said on a long, deep sigh that suddenly made him aware of her breasts, "it's a nice dream anyway. The important things, though, are spending time with one's children, saving for their education, making sure they're properly clothed and sheltered.'' She looked at him. "Don't you agree?''

He sensed she was testing him. "Of course, children should always come first.'' Had he really said that? He'd never voiced that opinion before, but he felt he really meant it at that moment.

Tyler took a quick swallow of the chilled pink wine and studied her expression, focused so intently on his. He knew she was fighting her innate shyness to hold her gaze steady. Maybe she had more backbone than he'd at first realized.

Their meals arrived, breaking their eye lock. After they'd both refused an offer of freshly ground pepper, he cut a large bite from his thick prime rib and tried to clear his head as he chewed. If he was seriously considering marrying this woman, there must be other questions he should ask.

"Did you get your thrifty nature from your parents?''

He watched with alarm as the glow drained from her cheeks. "I'm sorry. I hit a nerve?"

Julie pursed her lips and pushed her fork gently into a fat sea scallop. "I don't remember my mother. She left my father and me before I was a year old. Dad didn't have much of a head for budgets. He drove trucks all of his life, never made much money. As soon as I was old enough to shop for us, I made sure there was food to last through the end of every month."

Tyler frowned. "I see."

"It wasn't a bad life, but I spent a lot of time alone. My father passed away four years ago. I've lived on my own since. My aunts, uncles and cousins all live on the East Coast. I rarely get to see them."

Tyler imagined her as a child. A waif with stringy brown hair and no responsible adult to look after her. He could imagine her balled up in a chair in a corner of the children's reading room, lost in a fairy tale. It suited her.

He felt a pang of guilt for all he'd had and taken for granted. Sure, Devlin had worked most of the time. Tyler had desperately yearned for his father's attention, but never had it crossed his mind that his next meal might not appear when he was hungry.

He looked into Julie's eyes and saw an eternity of loneliness. He didn't need to ask why she wanted a family now. But there was one thing he didn't understand. "Your profile said you are twenty-seven years old."

"Yes." She tipped her head to one side, waiting, her fork poised over her meal.

"If you've always wanted to start a family, why haven't you married before now?"

With a little huff, she deliberately laid her fork across her plate and looked up at him as if he'd just slapped her. "Are you trying to make fun of me, Tyler?"

He gasped. "No, of course not, I—"

"Look at me," she demanded.

He looked. What he saw was a charming burst of fire in her eyes. But he didn't know if he was meant to see that or something else, so he kept quiet.

"I'm no catch. I fade into walls, don't have much of a figure, wear clothes because they're comfortable, not fashionable. I get nervous on dates and make lousy small talk. I freeze up when a man tries to kiss me. I—"

"You cook," he interrupted. "And you reupholster furniture and love books."

"Yes," she agreed on a long outward breath, eyeing him suspiciously.

"And you're not nearly as ordinary as you seem to think. You have lovely eyes, Julie. When you laugh or get angry, like now, they light up to put an acetylene torch to shame."

"Is that construction humor?" she asked dryly.

"No, it's the truth. Which you should recognize because you seem to be an honest person yourself." He reached out and laid his hands over hers on the white linen tablecloth, then held them there when she made a weak effort to pull away. "Although you're quiet, you speak up when something is important to you. You're intelligent, which can be very sexy to any man with half a brain. And you won't drive a man into bankruptcy by expecting lavish gifts. That seems to me the sort of woman a lot of men would be wise to consider as a wife."

Julie stared at Tyler Fortune. Did she dare believe he was serious? A man as stunningly sexy and self-possessed as he, telling her she was...what? Desirable? No, maybe not that, because he hadn't even hinted that she aroused him. No, it was more as if he recognized her few strong qualities and acknowledged he might look favorably upon them in choosing a partner. But that was far more than any other man had ever given her.

"Thank you," she murmured. "It means a lot that you'd say something so kind to me."

"You deserve at least that." Before she could react, he lifted her right hand and brought it toward him across the table. His lips brushed her fingertips so lightly she barely felt their touch. He sandwiched her quivering hand between his two rough, warm palms. "Listen, I understand why you want to marry. Families are important. Actually, if you decide to go through with this matchmaking thing, I have a rather large clan to share with you."

Her heart leapt into her throat and an irrational joy filled her. He sounded serious. Until this moment, she hadn't believed, not deep down in her soul, that he'd want her.

"Your family," she said, forgetting all about her dinner, "what are they like?"

He looked a little unsure of himself. "I'll be more than happy to describe them to you. But first, in all fairness, I should clear up a few misconceptions you might have about me."

Her rainbow of hope faded. "Misconceptions?"

"You see," he began, "when I told you I was in construction, I think you sort of read into the term and—"

"That's all right," she interrupted. "The job doesn't make the man. Even if you dig ditches for a living, as long as you're honest and work hard for your money, we'll make do."

"No." He smiled boyishly at her. "I'm at the other end on the economic ladder."

"You mean," she said slowly, trying to make sense of what he was saying. "You mean, you're a crew boss...or a *foreman?* How wonderful, Tyler, I'm so proud of you!" She bounced on her chair in spontaneous delight but stopped herself when the couple at the nearest table turned to smile in her direction.

"I own the company. And it's a big one."

She stared blankly at him. "You what?"

Turning her hand palm up, as if to read her future, he explained casually, "Actually I share ownership with my parents, brother and cousins. I guess you've never heard of Fortune Construction. Most people don't pay attention to the names of builders, even on big projects. I'll bet there aren't ten people in all of Houston who could tell you who built the Astrodome."

Her free hand flew to her mouth. "No."

"No, what?" His gray eyes darkened with uncertainty.

"You're one of *those* Fortunes? Last week I read in the newspaper about a wealthy Native American family that was building a children's hospital somewhere in Arizona."

"That's us." Tyler grinned, looking smug.

Her heart sank. This was terrible. Not only was the man handsome, sexy and intelligent, he was rich. There was only one possible explanation for his having anything to do with her. He must be mentally unhinged.

Julie felt like running out of the elegant dining room, straight to her car—if she could find it—and driving as fast as she could away from Tyler Fortune. She closed her eyes, fighting down the panic. But his deep voice called her back, and she focused again on his words.

"It isn't just the family," Tyler was saying. "A lot of donations have gone into the building fund. People who care all over the country are helping out."

She frowned. "This doesn't make sense. You must have money to burn. You could marry any woman you want."

"I don't want just any woman for a wife," he stated, but no warmth was directed at her.

"Then someone special. Like that woman over there."

Julie turned and gestured with the tip of her chin toward a woman sitting at a nearby table. "She's stunning. Just look at her—perfectly styled blond hair, beautiful jewelry…and that dress." She sighed and leaned across the table to whisper. "Do you realize, Tyler, she's been staring at you since we came into this room? I'll bet women are always looking at you like that."

He shrugged as if he was too accustomed to attention from the opposite sex to be surprised. "Look at the problem of marriage from my point of view. What if that woman there or some other agrees to become my wife because she's physically attracted to me? How will she feel about me five years from now? Or, if money is the object of her affection, will she be calculating even before our wedding day how much alimony she can grab?"

"But surely, there are attractive women who might genuinely—"

"Fall in love with me? Be willing to take me on for better or worse in the traditional sense?" There was a heavy touch of bitterness in his laugh. "Haven't stumbled across any yet, lady."

"I see." She sighed.

"Why are you trying to talk me out of marrying you?"

She dared a quick glimpse of his smoky eyes. She could lose herself in them, if she stayed there too long. He definitely wasn't a lounge lizard; he was clever, charming and far more dangerous. She retrieved her hand from between his. "I don't know. Maybe it's because I feel this is too good to be true. I can't believe you'd choose me over a woman like…like that."

Tyler followed her glance back to the stunning blonde. "Most of what she has to offer can be bought, inserted, painted on or surgically augmented."

Julie stifled a giggle in spite of her anxiety. "You're wicked."

"You've found me out."

He had her laughing now, and it was so delightful he was determined to make her continue. But first he had to lay his cards on the table. "Listen, I won't lie to you. I have an ulterior motive for wanting to marry right away." Her eyes went from twinkling to enormous and apprehensive. "It has to do with Fortune Construction and keeping my share of my grandfather Ben's company. My parents have told me that if I'm not married by my birthday, I don't inherit."

"But—" Julie shook her head in disbelief "—but that's not fair!"

"Fair or not, they've decided their youngest son needs a settled family life to be happy and ensure the continuation of the company in the family."

"Let me guess…they've come up with their own list of suitable mates for you?"

He nodded. "Plenty of local gals. But I don't want anyone choosing a wife for me. And no one I've dated is the kind of woman I could live with for the rest of my life."

"But I am?" she asked incredulously.

He let his eyes drift over her soft features. "I think you might be. Your needs are simple, and as long as we understand one another from the start, we should be able to come to some sort of agreement that's beneficial to both of us. If it helps, consider this purely a business relationship."

She nodded slowly. "It sounds terribly cold, but I think I could do that. I had already come to terms with fairy tales when I contacted Soulmate Search."

"Fairy tales?" he asked.

"You know...finding my true love, if such a thing exists. I'm a realist, Tyler."

She looked him dead in the eyes and he felt an unexpected jolt down low in his gut. Something akin to arousal. She isn't my type, he reminded himself. Not my type at all.

"About the sex," she whispered.

"What?" Had he heard her right? He looked around but no one at the nearby tables seemed to have heard.

"You know—intercourse." She blushed at her own breathy words.

He stopped himself from smiling at her embarrassment and tried to look serious. "Yes?"

"You'll need to sleep with me if I'm to conceive."

"I expect so."

"Well, since we're being up front about everything...I just want you to know that you don't have to...that is, you don't have to do *it* any more often than is necessary."

"I see." Did she think he'd be relieved to hear this? Her words had the opposite effect on him. He suddenly wanted to know how she'd look stripped of her pert sweater set and tidy wool skirt. He felt himself move and shifted in his chair to compensate for the tightness across his lap.

Time to change topics.

"We'll deal with that when the time comes," he said quickly. "Meanwhile, I want you to meet my family and see Pueblo, my hometown, before you make a decision."

"You should be sure of me, too," she insisted.

"I will be soon enough. I don't take long to make up my mind about things."

She took a last bite of her seafood and pushed away her plate, even though it was still half full of shrimp, scallops and delicate lumps of white crabmeat swimming in its buttery sauce. "I'm free this weekend." She looked up at him guilelessly. "That is, if you want me to come to Pueblo then."

"Perfect."

"What will you tell your parents about me? Do they know about Soulmate?"

"Hell, no." He chuckled at the thought. "And they don't need to know. They'll be shocked as it is if we go through with this." He thought for a moment. "I'll have to tell them we've known each other for a while, if you don't mind."

"I'm not a very good liar," she warned.

"You don't have to lie. I'll cover for us with some simple excuse. You just be yourself."

She drew a deep breath that brought his gaze to her sweater again, stretched tightly where she pressed forward against the edge of the table. She had very nice breasts.

"Are you sure this arrangement of ours will be fair to them?"

"Huh?" He quickly looked up to connect with her concerned hazel eyes. "Why shouldn't it be?"

"I'm probably not what they're expecting."

"You're right, you're not." He leaned across the table, somehow avoiding plates and crystal. Before she had a chance to pull away, he'd kissed her on the mouth. "You're a damn sight better, Miss Julie Parker."

Julie thought about Tyler's kiss as she drove away from Van Gogh's that evening, and all of the next day at work. She figured it for a kind of good-luck kiss. Not much more than a friendly peck, a handshake, a deal-sealer.

Yet the warmth of his lips lingered on hers, making her think of a longer, deeper, more satisfying kiss that might be waiting for her. Some day.

But even such a pleasant thing as a kiss worried her. Tyler Fortune was a man whose entire life had been determined by his family from the day of his birth. This she had learned on her lunch hour.

She'd found several revealing newspaper articles. Tyler's grandfather, Ben, had moved to Arizona while separated from his wife, Kate. He must have believed their marriage was over, for he'd lived with a Native American woman for several years and they'd had twin boys together—Devlin and Hunter. Devlin was Tyler's father, Hunter was his uncle. It wasn't until Natasha Lightfoot, Ben's mistress, died that Kate recognized Devlin and Hunter as Ben's children and agreed to give control of Ben's construction company to them when they turned twenty-five. Ben died soon thereafter.

Julie found photos of the family in the society pages of the Arizona newspapers. Articles in the business section traced the Fortunes' climb to power, year after year. Their most recent project was the multi-million Fortune Memorial Children's Hospital, situated between the Papago Indian Reservation and the smaller San Xavier Reservation. Julie gradually built for herself an image of a modern dynasty-in-the-making that took her breath away.

This man had so much to give her—a proud heritage, wealth, the babies she longed for. But what did she have to offer him?

That was the question that haunted her. Why me? She'd asked him that question, but he hadn't really given her a satisfactory answer. Everyone had a reason for the things they did. What was Tyler's?

Yet, as the day wore on and her question remained unanswered, she found she didn't want to dwell on it. Dining with Tyler at the trendiest restaurant in the city had been the most exciting evening of her life. As a child, the only restaurants she'd set foot in were fast-food joints. In high school she'd kept pretty much to herself. In college she'd dated a few young men who had sprung for a meal at a steak house.

But oh…how she'd loved sitting across a table from Tyler. When she'd left Van Gogh's her head had been reeling with the richness of the place. She'd felt such a pale daisy beside the rose-and-poppy opulence of the people sitting at the other tables in the intimate dining room.

And Tyler was the most amazing of them all. He had a rough-and-tumble physique that had let her easily assume he drove a forklift for a living until he'd told her otherwise. His face was tanned and sun-leathered, but strong and full of laughter when she said something that amused him. She liked amusing him. She bathed in the glow of his smiles.

"What do you want from me, Tyler Fortune?" she whispered as she climbed into her bed that night. She yawned and closed her eyes. "And what will you make me pay to get what I want from you?"

Three

___

Julie had never flown in an airplane. As she stood on the sunbaked tarmac Friday afternoon, staring doubtfully at the Fortune family's private jet, she decided the expense of flying wasn't the only good reason for keeping one's feet on the ground. To her dismay, the plane was so small it looked almost like a toy. This seemed a risky means of introducing herself to air travel.

But the flight was deliciously smooth, and it wasn't long before she sank comfortably into the rich leather seat the pilot had shown her to and released herself to drifting through billowy white clouds into a blue sky so clear and shockingly lovely she couldn't help sighing. Julie found herself thinking of Tyler.

She remembered the finely drawn muscles visible in the backs of his hands as he'd laid them over hers. The corded line of his throat had risen above his crisp shirt collar. The rest of his body, she imagined, would be just as strong and lean and hard. Envisioning him without his clothes sent delicious chills through her. Her cheeks radiated heat as the plane began its descent.

"Get a grip," Julie whispered to herself.

But in her heart, she knew that was impossible. She was being swept along on an exhilarating adventure, and she had no idea what to do except to let whatever might happen, happen.

This won't last long, she reassured herself. *You might as well enjoy yourself.* Tyler or his parents would soon realize how terribly wrong she was for him. The Fortunes would pack her off to Houston by the end of the weekend, and that would be that.

But at least she'd have some pretty memories, if their evening at Van Gogh's was a taste of what was in store for her. Maybe fate had intended Tyler as a gift to last her a lifetime? A taste of romance. A memory to make her simple existence bearable. Maybe she should stop being afraid and just accept the weekend for what it was, pure fantasy.

When Julie stepped off the plane, she looked around the lonely airstrip for Tyler, her heart pounding in her chest, but he wasn't there. Instead, a short, middle-aged man wearing work clothes approached her. He smiled and held out a hand.

"Miss Parker? I'm Joe Dan White. I work for Mr. Fortune. He's sent me to fetch you."

"Oh," she said, feeling vaguely disappointed. No expectations, she warned herself. If you have no dreams, you can't feel cheated when they don't come true.

They drove in a battered sport utility vehicle with a pile of blueprints bouncing on the seat between them. Joe Dan wasn't a talkative man, but she didn't mind the silence. If he'd asked her what she was doing in Pueblo, she couldn't have given him an answer that made any sense.

Twenty minutes later, the truck stopped at a construction site beside a dusty silver trailer and Joe Dan jumped out of the cab. Julie hesitated before climbing down from the seat and took a moment to look around. Mountains rose on three sides, rough unforgiving crops of rock and scrub, but majestic in their own way.

"Mr. Fortune will be in the office over there," Joe Dan said, nodding toward the trailer as he scooped the blue-prints off the seat. "I have to drop these off with him. Come along, miss."

It occurred to her that Tyler hadn't explained who she was or why she was here. A second twinge of annoyance pinched at her. She set her shoulders and started toward the trailer.

But before Julie reached the metal steps, the door opened, and out stepped the man who had filled her mind for the past forty-eight hours. To her amazement, Tyler was even more striking in work clothes. Disturbingly so. His blue jeans molded smoothly around his lean hips and long legs. The top two pearl buttons of his western-style shirt were undone, and she could see a tuft of dark hair against a V of hard chest. Breathe, she told herself, feeling light-headed.

"How was your flight?" he asked, smiling down at her.

"Wonderful!" she blurted out. Suddenly, her annoyance with his lack of attention to her arrival seemed irrelevant. "The sky was so clear I was sure I could see California."

Tyler combed the fingers of one hand through a healthy thatch of dark hair to move it off his forehead. He observed her conservative navy suit and pumps with concern.

"Is something wrong?" she asked.

"That outfit is going to pick up dust awful easy. I'd

hoped to show you around town, a combination driving and walking tour. Did you bring anything more comfortable?''

Virtually all the clothes she owned were outfits suitable for the library, or for puttering around in her kitchen at home. Since she rarely went out socially, she didn't need dress clothes or upscale casual wear.

"I do have a pair of flats with me and a pantsuit."

"We'll have to find you something more appropriate than that."

She hoped he didn't expect her to buy a new outfit for the weekend. She had only twenty dollars on her, in case of an emergency, and she didn't want to blow her charge account any higher for clothing she wouldn't be able to wear after the weekend.

"I need to speak to some of my men before I leave. You can wait in the office or come along." He picked up a hard hat from a bench outside the trailer and offered it to her.

"I'd like to see the hospital," she said quickly, accepting the brilliant-yellow shell and dropping it onto her head.

"Suit yourself." He took a second hat for himself. "It will be difficult for you to imagine what the finished building will look like at this stage."

But she could imagine it so very easily. As they walked past a huge billboard stating that this was the Fortune Memorial Children's Hospital, she eyed the artist's rendition of the completed structure. A fountain and trees were enclosed by a circular drive in front of a central tower. Off one end was a fenced playground, and to the rear an emergency entrance for ambulances. The highest point of the structure was fifteen floors and the whole of it rose out of the desert like an enormous flowering cactus.

"It's going to be wonderful," she murmured appreciatively.

"I sure hope so." Tyler shook his head, thinking how far they'd come, yet how much further they had to go. "There are times I've worried it would never come together. But we're getting there, slowly."

"It must be wonderful, building a dream from the ground up. Making something out of nothing but hope."

The pure enthusiasm in her voice forced Tyler to look at her. Julie's eyes sparkled and her face glowed. That was how he felt on a good day. But those hadn't come often enough since Mike Dodd's death.

"My dad's favorite part of putting up a new building is breaking ground," Tyler murmured. "He says he feels something mystical when the first shovel of dirt is lifted. But I like this part—building the frame that shapes and supports the whole thing." He pointed. "We intentionally move some parts along more quickly. We're putting some glass into the lower floors of the west wing this week. It helps people visualize how it will turn out."

She smiled up at him. "That's nice, to think of folks that way."

"We have practical reasons, too," he said solemnly. "As important as this project is to the children of the region, we've had to fight to get it approved."

And Tyler Fortune was clearly a fighter. She could see his determination and courage sketched in the strong slashes of cheek and jawbone and the firm line of his lips. Astride a pinto, a lance raised in one hand, reins in the other, he'd have been a warrior worthy of any opponent.

Which brought to mind the question of how she might hope to survive the partnership he proposed. He'd suggested a simple business relationship. That was what she'd envisioned, too. But that was before she'd met Tyler. The husband she had been looking for was a quiet, undemanding man whose personality matched hers. Tyler was used to getting his way, and he was anything but retiring.

On the other hand, if he was serious about his proposition, and if she didn't take the risk now...she'd probably never have another chance at marriage or an honest-to-goodness adventure.

Tyler walked away from her to speak with several of his crew. Julie weighed her options while she pretended to study the sketch of the hospital. When he returned, nodding toward the trailer to indicate they could leave now, she stopped him with a timid touch on his forearm.

"What?"

"You're really serious about doing this—marrying me?"

"I wouldn't have asked you to come out here if I wasn't."

She sighed. "Tyler, you live in the center of an empire." He snorted and opened his mouth to object, but she held up a hand. "No, listen. Maybe that's not the right word, but this place, your employees, the children who will come here and your family—they all have a lot at stake in you. When you marry, you have to consider everyone, particularly your parents. It won't take them long to figure out I'm not part of their social network. You're using me to ensure your inheritance. They'll suspect I'm after your money. They'll hate me."

"Are you?"

"Am I what?"

He grinned. "After my money?"

Her mouth dropped open. Being with a man who said exactly what was on his mind took some getting used to. She forced herself to meet his steady gaze. "No. All I want is a family. I was ready to accept any decent, hardworking man.''

''Then you're not after my body either?'' His smile barely lifted the corners of his mouth.

He was teasing her, and she bridled. ''Sex is overrated.''

Now he looked intrigued, challenged. And that was far worse. That was dangerous. ''Really,'' he drawled. ''And you've made an in-depth study of the topic, Miss Parker?''

Julie shifted from one foot to the other then back to the first. She looked away from him, unable to meet his wolf-ish gray eyes. ''I—I don't know how we got on to this subject,'' she stammered, hoping none of his crew was close enough to hear their words.

''Forgive me, but I tend to connect the two—marriage and intimate relations. If we're going to live together it's only right that I give up dating other women. Wouldn't you agree?''

''Well, I—''

''In which case, I'd say that you, as my legal wife, will have an obligation—'' He lifted one dark brow heavy with meaning ''—to satisfy me.''

Her throat was suddenly so parched she couldn't get a word out for several seconds.

''I, um…I thought we agreed that intimacy would be necessary to create our family, but we wouldn't sleep together otherwise.''

''I don't believe I agreed to any such thing,'' he said calmly, watching her with an intensity that unnerved her even more.

''And I don't believe I mentioned at any time playing the role of your…your *love slave!*'' she exclaimed.

He laughed gustily and long, and kept on laughing until he had to wipe tears from his eyes. Several burly men nearby turned to watch them. Julie felt her cheeks flush with heat. "Well, it sounds as if that's what you expect," she hissed at him, and spun toward the trailer.

"Slave. Love slave…" He couldn't stop the aftershocks of chuckles as he followed her. "Is that how you view your role in a relationship with a man? You'd be expected to do unpleasant things to please him as a price for being given children?"

She squeezed her eyes shut, still walking. "Please don't make a scene."

"Make a scene?"

Julie felt close to tears. Her head felt so clogged with confusing emotions, she couldn't think straight. All she knew was that she wanted to escape from Tyler Fortune and the feelings he churned up inside her.

"I think," Tyler said in a firm voice, "we had better get a few things straight before either of us makes a decision about this arrangement." He took her firmly by the arm and pulled her the rest of the way across the raw stretch of ground and up the metal steps.

Tyler had no clue what he'd do or say once he got Julie out of sight of his obviously amused crew. Did this woman expect him to marry her but live the life of a celibate? On the one hand he couldn't help feeling sorry for her, as naive as she was. On the other, he didn't feel sorry enough to let her dictate a passionless future for him.

"The only way this might…just might work," he said, and forced himself to release her, "is if we're honest with each other. Completely honest. Can you agree to that much?"

She nodded meekly.

"Good, that's a beginning." Tyler paced the narrow office while she stood trembling near the door, her eyes darting wistfully toward it as he spoke.

"I'll start," he said, then took a long breath. "My per-

sonal choice would be to remain single. Seeing as that's
not possible, I'm dealing with the situation. The problem
is, I take marriage seriously. If I didn't, I could marry
anyone, work my twelve-hour days, sleep with other
women and hardly ever have to see Mrs. Tyler Fortune.''

''I see,'' she murmured, her eyes enormous.

''But that's not me, Julie. I know I'll have to make some
sacrifices—spend a little less time on the job to be with
my kids and treat the woman I marry honorably. I couldn't
do otherwise. Understand so far?''

She nodded, allowing him a faint smile.

Now came the hard part, the part that might send her
scurrying out the door and out of his life. The part he
hadn't intended to tell her. ''I didn't choose you randomly
from Soulmate's videotapes. I saw something in you I felt
I could live with, a quality of womanhood that appealed
to me.''

''Maybe you just saw a woman you could control.'' She
barely breathed the words.

Yes, he thought, there was that, too. She'd come too
damn close to the other side of the coin. He stepped closer
and lifted a strand of her hair between his first finger and
thumb. ''I don't want to control you.'' He wound the delicate filaments around his finger, and, despite his reassuring words, suddenly felt the urge to tug her still closer.
Maybe controlling her physically would be interesting.
''All I meant was, something about your interview touched
me.''

Her body tensed. She lifted her eyes to meet his.

''And now that you're really here,'' he said, ''not just
an image on a TV screen, there's something very pleasing
about you, Julie Parker. I'd like to sleep with you and
figure out what that something is, because it's driving me
nuts.''

Through the ends of her hair he could feel her quiver in response to his words. He wondered if her reaction was due to fear or excitement. He hoped with all that was in him that it was the second of the two.

"Is that the way you relate to all women?" she asked timidly. "You have sex with them?"

"Not always." He couldn't help tossing her a wicked grin. Maybe he shouldn't tease her when she seemed so vulnerable, but he had to break the ice somehow. Besides, playfully tormenting a woman was damn good fun. "Does that bother you, thinking about me making love to another woman?"

"No!" She came back at him so quickly it seemed to surprise even her. "I mean…why should it concern me at all?"

"I would hope that any woman I married would take her husband's fidelity seriously." An amazing thought occurred to him. "It would bother me if I discovered you with another man."

She looked more curious now than afraid. "It would? Why?"

"I tend to be somewhat possessive by nature." He shrugged. Maybe that was all there was to it.

"And if we married, you'd feel that you owned me. Is that it?"

"Not owned you." Tyler turned her toward him and settled his hands on her shoulders. "I suppose I'd be hurt to think I hadn't satisfied you." He wasn't sure where these confessions were coming from, but they weren't as painful as he might have expected. He was accustomed to speaking his mind, not his emotions. Maybe because he sensed how fragile Julie was, he didn't feel vulnerable.

"Oh," she said, her expression opening up as if she were a flower turning toward the sun.

"Listen, I'm not promising I could ever love you. But if it happened, in time, I guess it would be something I could accept. It would fit with our circumstances, right?"

"Right," she whispered, gazing up at him with such trust and openness, he could do nothing less than kiss her.

She didn't back away when he ducked his head. It wasn't until her soft features swam out of focus that he realized this kiss wasn't going to be tentative, comforting or particularly gentle. She started to flinch, but it was too late. His wide hand found the back of her neck. His fingers combed up through the wisps of hair, anchoring around strands at the nape to be certain she couldn't draw away even if she tried.

He held her motionless while his mouth covered hers, then parted her lips. He tasted her as intimately as though they'd done this a dozen times before. He'd kissed scores of women. They'd all responded with enthusiasm, and he had felt carbon-copy male reactions to them. But this time it was different. Maybe it was the promises they were making to each other. Whatever the reason, he felt as if he was claiming Julie Parker as his own. Not just for the moment…for forever.

He took his time, savoring her lips, plunging between them, holding her and stroking her throat until she felt limp and compliant in his arms. He didn't particularly want to let her go. But there was no guarantee of privacy in the thin-walled trailer.

When at last he stepped away to look down at Julie, her lips were slightly swollen and her eyes bore a distant, dreamy expression. "Why did you—" she swallowed, caught her breath "—do that?"

"Testing for potential." He was trying for casual wit, but his voice sounded hoarse and strained. He cleared his throat. "Care to know the results?"

She blinked at him, looking afraid to ask.

"I'd say it's definitely there, Miss Parker."

She smiled.

He touched a fingertip to her lips and gazed down at her, feeling a foreign tenderness for this petite brunette. But he kept his face a blank. It wouldn't do to let her know how much she moved him. They were still in the negotiation stage. Important issues had to be settled.

"I think we've reached the time when we should talk about our personal histories," he said.

"But I told you that my parents—oh…" Julie belatedly read the message in his eyes. "*That* kind of history." She moved a step back from him and pressed a hand to the top of his desk, as if checking to make sure it would hold her, then perched on one corner. "I guess you can tell I've had less experience than you. I know I can make a nice home for you, love your children and care for them. But I'm not—" she lifted one thin shoulder then let it drop "—I just hope you're not expecting me to be like those women in the movies who drive a man crazy in thirteen different positions."

This time there was no way he could stop himself from smiling so hard his cheeks hurt. She was adorable. "You don't have to worry about that."

"But—"

He quieted her lips with another tap of his finger. "I'll show you everything you'll need to know to please me, Julie. And I'll never force you to make love with me. It has to be something you want, too. I'm counting on our hungers being mutual."

Her eyes slid away from his, to the floor. "I'm not a very…responsive person."

"I don't believe that."

"You said I should be honest with you. I'm trying to be," she insisted sadly.

"If you say so." He couldn't believe that the woman he'd felt melting in his arms moments earlier wouldn't share his passion if she were given the chance. He reached out and cupped her cheek in his hand. She couldn't seem to look at him now. "Come on, living with me isn't the worst possible fate, is it?"

She shook her head and gave him a weak smile. "Not at all," she murmured.

"So," he said watching her expression hopefully. "Do we do this?"

She lifted her gaze to meet his, looked deep into his eyes and nibbled anxiously at her bottom lip. He wished he could read her thoughts at that moment, but he doubted even she had yet made sense of the muddle of doubts, needs, fears and dreams he saw reflected in her expressive hazel eyes.

When he was sure her hesitation meant she'd decided against his plan, she let out a soft breath of resignation and murmured a single word he only half heard.

"What?" he asked, his heart beat rising to a rapid tattoo.

Julie blinked up at him. "Yes," she said more clearly. "Yes, I'll marry you."

The morning passed into afternoon before Julie knew it. Once she'd given Tyler her decision, he seemed determined to introduce her to every landmark in town. Pueblo wasn't anywhere near as large as Tucson, but it was big enough for its own shopping mall (a very exclusive one it appeared to Julie), a fifties'-style diner called the Copper Mine and a local steak house whimsically known as the Camel Corral. Tyler described this last establishment as a "guy hangout." He and his brother Jason still met there at least once a week for a juicy sirloin and beer.

The headquarters of Fortune Construction took up most of an entire block along Feather Road. Tyler walked her through the main entrance and into his office on an upper floor. The corridors were lined with magnificent southwestern woven rugs and oil paintings of Tyler's ancestors. An original Remington bronze held an honored place in the central foyer.

Finally, they looped back through town in his pickup truck, past several churches, two bakeries, a large pharmacy positioned midtown and a smaller one close to the Saguaro Springs residential community of two-story Mediterranean-style condos and houses.

"That's where I live," he told her. "We'll come back in a while, but I'd like you to meet my parents first."

"So soon!" Julie gasped.

He grinned. "No time like the present. Don't worry, they don't eat Texans."

Julie studied Tyler's profile as he turned the truck down a private road then steered between a graceful row of poplar trees dressed in new green leaves. He was a proud redwood of a man; she a spindly willow. He made heads turn when he entered a room; she could pass through without anyone realizing she'd been there. How would she ever survive in his shadow?

Tyler stopped the car at a wrought-iron gate, rolled down his window to punch a code into a keypad. The tall, scrolled panels, each emblazoned with a large *F*, swung open. Some five hundred feet down the drive was a rambling ranch-style home of stucco and red tile, as close to a mansion as she'd ever seen on one floor.

"Is this where you grew up?" she asked.

"Yes. My parents live here now, and my grandmother

Kate has been visiting from Minneapolis for the winter. Sterling, who she married several years ago, is away on business for a few weeks. But with any luck my brother or cousins will drop in for supper.''

With any luck, Julie thought with trepidation. She was anxious enough about meeting Tyler's parents without having to make a grand appearance before his entire family.

Tyler flung open a door at the end of the house without knocking. "Anyone home?" he called out, his voice booming through the big house.

"In the living room, Ty," a soft voice answered.

Julie looked at Tyler. "You have a sister, too?"

"That's my mother, Jasmine. She'll be thrilled to hear you thought she sounded like a twenty-something. Come on, don't look so terrified." He chuckled.

Watching cool pinky-gray slabs of marble flooring pass beneath her feet, Julie tried to think what she would say to the mother of her fiancé—for that was what Tyler was to her now. Her fiancé. The concept both excited and terrified her. *Glad to meet you, Mrs. Fortune. I've known your son for less than one full day, and I've decided to marry him.* Would a sane woman be doing this?

Yet Tyler seemed a very practical man who didn't leap blindly into ventures. If he believed they could marry for their mutual benefit and make it work, why shouldn't she also believe? After all, he'd had a lot more experience with relationships than she.

They rounded a corner and stepped into a spacious parlor decorated in cream, rust and a spectrum of tans with touches of turquoise—southwestern motif and colors. The room was twice as large as her entire apartment, with dark wood beams holding aloft a soaring cathedral ceiling and a stone fireplace that occupied the entire far wall. A couple sat on a love seat, close enough to hold hands without reaching. The man was tall, thin and strong looking. His hair was beginning to gray around the temples. Julie immediately saw a strong resemblance to Tyler. Chiseled stone, a warrior's proud nose and watchful eyes.

On seeing her son enter the room with a woman on his arm, Jasmine looked puzzled. An older woman sitting across from Tyler's parents turned to smile graciously at them. Her hair was a crisp white, arranged in swirls around her face. Her eyes were sharp and blue when they shifted toward Julie. This must be Kate, the matriarch of the clan, Julie thought.

Kate seemed instinctively to know how to fill the awkward moment. "Ah, what a lovely surprise. You've brought a friend, Tyler dear. Are you two staying for dinner?"

"If there's enough to go around." He vigorously tugged Julie farther into the room when she balked, and pinned her to his side with one strong arm.

"Grand! We'll have a small crowd then. Jason and Adele are also expected, bringing little Lisa, of course. I love it when the brood gets together around the same table." She winked at Julie. "It doesn't happen often enough in this family, everyone is so busy. And who is this pretty creature with you?"

Julie felt the muscles in Tyler's arm tighten even though his expression remained amazingly relaxed.

"Everyone, this is Julie Parker, an old friend. We ran into each other again just recently in Houston. She lives there."

Tyler completed introductions all around. It was all Julie could do to nod shyly at the threesome and murmur something vague about being pleased to be in Pueblo.

"It's strange," Jasmine said, a note of apology in her voice, "I don't recall hearing about you before, Julie."

"I don't introduce all my dates to you, Mother," Tyler said smoothly.

"You don't introduce *any* of them to us," his grandmother corrected him. She turned to Julie with a gracious smile. "You must be a very special young woman to have earned the honor. You're not his usual sort of companion, thank goodness. I approve entirely."

"Thank you." Julie smothered a nervous laugh behind her hand. It was easy to see where Tyler got his no-nonsense manner of dealing with people.

"This is a lovely house," Julie said. "Is it very old?"

"My husband built it for the family," Kate explained. "Devlin and Hunter were already teenagers. Hunter lived here until he married. Devlin has never left, and Jason and Tyler grew up here." She looked around her at the stucco walls and heavy, dark beams overhead with love in her eyes. "I hope that Tyler, Jason or one of their cousins will have it some day. I would hate for it to be sold out of the family." She looked pointedly at her son, then her grandson.

"That's understood, Mother," Devlin assured her affectionately.

Kate's sharp eyes flicked back to Julie. "We're having drinks while we wait for the others to arrive. Sit here and tell us about yourself, Julie." She patted the long stretch of sofa beside her.

It was more a command than a request. Julie accepted a glass of white zinfandel and sat between Kate and Tyler on a plump, sand-colored cushion. He slipped his arm around her waist. She tensed for an instant before reminding herself it would seem odd if her fiancé didn't display a gesture of affection. She eased back against his arm and sipped her wine, trying to look as if she was accustomed to visiting the wealthy and concocting outrageous tales about herself.

"There isn't a lot that's very interesting," she began, hoping they wouldn't pursue the topic if she sounded bored with it herself. "I work for the Houston Public Library system. I was born in southwest Houston and grew up there. I've never really left."

Kate's eyes widened. "You're a librarian? How wonderful. I hope all my great-grandchildren will be avid readers, but I fear these computer games and movies...." She rolled her eyes.

"Children still read a lot. Educational Internet sites actually encourage children to seek out traditional books." Julie warmed to her topic at the spark of interest in Kate's eyes.

She caught a glimpse of Tyler watching her with a curious expression, and suddenly realized she was talking with a great deal more animation than at any time since she'd met him. He looked amused, thoughtful and a little less sure of himself.

The time passed quickly. Jasmine told her about Tyler's cousin Shane, who was an expert in Native American cultures. Kate assured her that Shane would want to consult with her about research he was doing on the Papago tribe. And when Jasmine eventually brought up the subject of Julie's family, she was able to answer honestly. "Families are terribly important to me. I'll be forever grateful I had my father as long as I did. But I always envied children who had a bevy of brothers and sisters."

She noticed Jasmine and Kate swapping hopeful looks. Tyler took this as his cue.

"Before the others arrive, I'd like to make an announcement." He glanced down at Julie, as if for approval, but she knew nothing short of a Texas twister would stop him. All she could do was play along.

"Whatever you think is best, darling," she murmured.

Tyler's parents and grandmother stared at him…then her…then him again. Pulling Julie closer, Tyler planted a noisy kiss on the crest of her head. Although she understood this was part of the act, a ripple of heat spread down through her body—like sweet maple syrup slowly poured.

"Nothing ever happens in this family in the expected way," Tyler began. "You three have been after me for years to get serious, settle down with one woman, marry and start a family. But I've always had the feeling I hadn't met the right woman. I was wrong."

Julie let her eyes float shut for a moment, trying to borrow strength from the protective circle of Tyler's arms. His family had treated her graciously, believing she was just another of his dates. Now came the moment when they would tell her she wasn't worthy of him and throw her out of their home.

Her fingers felt ice-cold. Her right foot had been so tightly wedged beneath her knee on the couch cushion, it had fallen asleep. She grimaced, tried flexing her toes, but pins and needles danced up her leg. She desperately wanted the next five minutes to be over.

Oblivious to Julie's emotional and physical discomfort, Tyler wove a tale of their brief courtship while nuzzling his chin into the nest of curls atop her head. "I didn't recognize how special Julie was when we dated years ago. It wasn't until we ran into each other again that it became obvious to me—she is the woman I want to marry."

Julie arranged a semblance of a smile on her lips and watched her future in-laws' shocked expressions gradually mellow to pleasure, while Tyler continued creating their love story out of thin air. His Julie had utterly charmed him with her sweet gentleness. He was as smitten by her gourmet cooking as he was by her intelligence. They agreed on so many issues…including having children.

Actually, everything but his feelings for her were the absolute truth. And she almost believed even those parts.

By the time Jason arrived with his new wife, Adele, and his daughter Lisa, dinner was on the table and everyone was congratulating the happy couple, offering Julie words of encouragement and welcome into the clan. Julie was stupefied. Had they actually bought it? The proof seemed to be that she was still standing in their home, being hugged and kissed by everyone, including the cook, who seemed a member of the family.

Jason offered a toast at the beginning of the meal then leaned across the table with a solemn expression. "You're not going to turn cheap on your fiancée, are you, Ty?"

Tyler scowled at him. "What are you talking about?"

"I don't see a diamond on that pretty lady's finger."

Julie sensed Tyler's momentary loss for an explanation. Words rushed out of her mouth before she could consider what she was saying. "That's because I asked him to wait."

Tyler stared at her. "You did, yes," he said slowly, buying time while he tried to figure out where she was headed, "because…"

"Because I wanted him to tell his family first."

"Ah, yes." He picked up the story, shooting her a thankful look. "Silly woman thought there might be an objection to her. Lord only knows why. I told her you'd all adore her."

"You still should have offered Julie a ring," Jasmine scolded her son. "It's traditional, Tyler. Sometimes, I swear you think you can make up your own rules as you go along in life."

"Mother, I didn't—"

Julie came to his rescue a second time. "I asked that we pick out a ring together. I was afraid he'd choose a huge, gaudy stone. My hands are so small, I look silly in big jewelry."

Kate laughed, pressing a damask napkin to her lips. "My dear, a woman can never have a diamond that's too big. My advice to you is to pick out the largest perfect diamond my grandson can afford, and, believe me, that's a whopper. He's had plenty of time to save up for it!"

Julie returned the older woman's conspiratorial smile. "I'll remember that when we visit the jeweler tomorrow." She glanced with innocent sweetness at Tyler.

"Tomorrow?" he asked, dark brows lowering.

"Tomorrow," Julie repeated, proud that her voice didn't quaver. Maybe the courage came from the wine. Or maybe it was the way Adele was viewing her approvingly from across the table.

"Good, now that that is settled," Kate rolled on joyfully, "you two need to set a date, arrange for a church, choose a cake and photographer, order flowers—"

"Can I be the flower girl?" Little Lisa bounced on her chair. "I'll practice real hard."

"That's Julie's decision," Kate said briskly. "As is the location of the wedding. Do you have a church in mind?"

"Well, no," Julie replied. "I just assumed since Tyler has a big family and mine is so small, and distant, we'd be married in Pueblo."

"Wonderful!" Kate exclaimed. "The reception will, of course, be here at the house."

Tyler was shaking his head emphatically. "Julie and I have agreed on a very small, simple wedding. With work on the hospital running behind schedule and losing my foreman, I don't have time for—"

"You don't have time for your own wedding?" Jasmine cried. "Oh, Tyler."

"Julie doesn't want a lot of fuss either," he insisted. "Do you, darling?"

Everyone turned to her.

"Aren't we going to have a wedding?" Lisa asked plaintively.

Julie looked up into Tyler's dark eyes, by now close to black. He was definitely a man not to be crossed.

"Isn't that right, sweetheart?" he asked again, more tightly.

She dared not push her luck. "Ah...yes," she whispered. "Just a simple ceremony." But she couldn't help feeling the sting of disappointment. Flowers, stained glass, a huge celebration! What fun it would have been. "The town hall will be just fine," she added.

"Well, I won't hear of it!" Kate fairly bellowed, flinging her napkin on the tabletop as if it were a gauntlet tossed down in challenge. "You'd better not let your son have his way with this, Devlin. Every girl deserves a formal wedding. Tell him he can't run off with this sweet little thing to a sterile clerk's office to take her vows. That's not fair."

Devlin didn't get a chance to speak.

"Of course he won't do that—will you Tyler?" Jasmine's glare, Julie thought, could easily have melted one of his steel girders.

"Well, I—" Tyler rolled his eyes in defeat.

"Julie," Kate interrupted smoothly, as if everything had now been settled, "I know a precious shop in The Mall in Saguaro Valley that carries one-of-a-kind wedding gowns. Any style you can imagine. Your gown will be my gift to you. We'll shop tomorrow afternoon, after you and Tyler pick out the ring." She shot her grandson a challenging look. "I will want to see it. And while we're choosing your gown, Tyler can call the church and arrange a date."

"But it could take months before there's an opening," he objected.

The room went silent. Jason coughed diplomatically. "I take it this isn't going to be a long engagement?"

"Well," Tyler said awkwardly, "Julie and I were thinking we wanted to get married next week. Not that we have to for the reason you're thinking."

"Next week," his grandmother repeated dryly. "Do you realize how long it takes to have invitations engraved? To book a caterer? And you must give guests enough warning to make plans."

Tyler glared at his family as if he'd lost his patience with all of them. "Listen, if you want to buy her a gown, see us hitched in a church and plan a big bash, go for it. But I'm telling you I don't have the time to fool around with elaborate wedding plans."

"What about you, Julie?" Kate turned to her across the table. "How do you feel?"

Julie took a moment to compose herself. "I just want to marry Tyler and start my new life," she said softly. It was, after all, the truth. "I don't need an expensive ceremony. It's not necessary for you all to go to a lot of trouble for me."

For a while no one spoke. Although Tyler was observing her with approval, she sensed that others at the table were wondering why she was letting Tyler stomp all over a woman's traditional right to an elaborate wedding when money wasn't an issue.

At last, Kate broke the silence. "I'll call the pastor myself and see if he can squeeze you two in sometime within the next week. The flowers and photographer may be a little more difficult.'' She glanced down the table to Adele. ''Are you up to the challenge, dear girl?''

Jason's pretty wife grinned, her green eyes flashing. ''After what you did for me? I'll follow you to Hades and back, Kate. Let's hit the phones after dinner.''

Before Julie could send Tyler a silent message that she was sorry he'd been stonewalled...even though she really wasn't, Kate caught her eyes. ''I'm so glad our Tyler found you, my dear. Don't you worry, this will work out just fine.''

Four

Tyler drove in silence away from the family estate. Julie felt his tension, but it couldn't have been any worse than her own. "I'm sorry," she said at last, fingering the electric window controls in the passenger door.

"What are you sorry for?" he grumbled.

"Back there…all that talk of the wedding. You're right. Maybe we should just elope." But feelings she hadn't expected had sprung up when Kate spoke of a gown and flowers and a church. It's all romantic fantasy, Julie told herself. Rainbow fluff. A soap-opera scene with lace and flowers and organ music, played over and over by centuries of brides.

Although it was obvious the Fortunes could afford such celebrations, it didn't seem right they should have to pay for one their son didn't even want! And what about the gown?

"I don't suppose we could talk your family out of this…this plan of theirs," she said with a sigh.

Tyler laughed dryly. "Not likely. Kate is the gang leader; she has no concept of defeat. I think the only way we're going to get married any time soon, without alienating my entire family, is by taking the path of least resistance."

"You mean, let your grandmother plan a formal wedding for us?"

He nodded somberly. "There will be hell to pay if we run off and get married without them." He turned to look at her. "I promise, once they get this out of their system, they'll only insist on the occasional family dinner. You can go back to your own routines, just as I will."

But her old hermitlike existence no longer had any appeal. Kate's sparkling eyes and energetic manner were contagious. Besides, dressing up like a bride might be fun!

"If it will make things easier," Julie said, trying to sound resigned to an unpleasant task, "I'll go along with whatever your family wants."

Tyler let out a long breath. "Thanks for being a good sport. I owe you one."

Julie turned her head away so that he wouldn't see the corners of her lips lift in a small, secret smile. How intriguing it was to contemplate Tyler Fortune owing her. She felt a wee bit wicked as she thought of the possibilities of collecting.

A moment later she was startled out of her daydreams when the truck turned into the Saguaro Springs residential area. "Oh. I thought you'd be taking me to the hotel. You did arrange for a room for me, didn't you?"

"My family knows me too well." He winked at her. "They'll expect we're already sleeping together."

"Of course." Her heart had somehow worked its way

up into her throat. "Um...what would happen if they discovered we hadn't already...you know...been intimate?"

"They'd know something was up. And they might find a way to stop the wedding."

"But you said they wanted you married."

"Happily married, to a woman they view as right for me. Luckily for us, you seem to fit the bill."

"I see. Is the reason they assume we're having sex because...well, if I'm not getting too personal, because you've slept with a lot of women?"

"I expect my reputation exceeds my deeds." He slanted her a meaningful look. "When you're considered the most eligible bachelor in all of Arizona, it pays to let people think you're a dedicated playboy. After a while, most husband-hunters give up the chase."

She giggled. "I see."

They pulled past a tennis club, private swimming pool, clubhouse and down another road through a rambling golf course. "There is a convenience store." He pointed out a small stucco structure. "For anything more than milk and bread, head for the mall. My father claims he built it for my mother. She's a shopping addict. He wanted to keep her closer to home."

Julie laughed. "That's a cute story."

"I'm pretty sure it's true." He parked in a numbered space, held the door to the condo open for Julie, then started switching on lights.

Standing in the middle of his living room, her overnight bag in hand, Julie turned her thoughts to the rest of the evening. A thousand questions bombarded her, not the least of which had to do with sleeping arrangements. She'd never in her life been alone with a grown man in his home. It felt dangerous, evocative...and ever so slightly delicious.

Tyler must have been on a similar wavelength, but perhaps in a more practical way. He pointed to the middle of the room. "That's a convertible sofa with a pull-out bed inside. I figured you'd probably want me to sleep out here, until we—"

"Thank you," she said quickly, glad for the privacy he was offering her. Nevertheless, she felt just a little disappointed. Ever since they'd agreed to this venture, her mind insisted upon conjuring up images of Tyler, sans clothing. Now, it would seem, she'd have to wait a while longer to see if reality lived up to her runaway imagination.

As for touching Tyler and being touched by him—that was something she couldn't allow herself to visualize just yet. It seemed impossible that he'd want her after having other women who already knew how to please a man. She was sure that when the time came she'd embarrass herself. Tyler would have to be patient, then take command of the situation.

But he seemed to enjoy taking charge of things and making decisions, so maybe it wouldn't turn out too awfully. Julie decided not to worry about that until the time came. And it would if she was to collect her part of the bargain. She might be naive, but she fully understood there was only one way to make a baby outside of a test tube.

"Thank you," she said. "I appreciate you giving up your bed for me."

There was a long pause and she only belatedly realized that Tyler was standing very still, observing her with such concentrated energy she felt his gaze as a smoldering sensation at the back of her neck. She turned to fully face him, and he suddenly stepped forward. Her right hand automatically shot up in front of her.

"I thought so," he said in a low voice.

"What?"

"You're afraid of me."

"I—I am not." Julie drew herself up straight and immediately retracted her hand.

"Your body language says you are. You tense up whenever I get too close. All the way here in the truck, you were as far to the right as the seat belt allowed. And now you look as if you're ready to bolt."

"You're exaggerating," she insisted. "I'm just a little nervous. Any woman planning to marry a stranger in less than a week would be."

A dangerous twinkle in his dark eyes warned her that his mood had turned playful again. "Maybe we'd better do something about that."

"What do you mean?" she asked suspiciously.

"I have a feeling that if we don't take active measures to relax my bride-to-be, she might not show up at the church."

"I promised to go through with this, and I will," she insisted through gritted teeth. The man was toying with her; she felt at a perilous disadvantage, not knowing what he was thinking.

"I'm not questioning your honest intentions." He moved forward cautiously, his lips lifting in a devilish smile. "I just think you need a chance to warm up to me."

Lord, help me, she thought. "If you're saying what I think you're saying—"

"Relax. If you don't want to consummate this relationship until after the ceremony, that's fine by me. But it's not natural to bottle up emotions the way you have for so long."

"My emotions are right where they belong," she retorted crisply. But she was so very curious. "What would you suggest?"

"Doctor Fortune suggests you change into something

comfortable, then enjoy a glass of wine with him in front of a blazing fire. Some therapeutic cuddling also might be in order.''

"And then?''

"Then…'' he flashed her a wicked smile "…as much or as little as you're ready for. It's up to you. At the very least, spending some time together will take the edge off. Believe me.''

"I don't know,'' she murmured doubtfully.

How could she tell Tyler that the more time she spent with him, the more vividly she fantasized about him? How could she admit that those mysteriously tantalizing fantasies were woven out of bits and pieces from movies, books and the gossip of other women? She had never done more than kiss a man, which was due as much to fear as to lack of opportunity.

"I promise,'' he said, reaching to take her hand in his, "nothing bad will happen, Julie.''

To her knowledge he hadn't deceived her yet. If she was going to commit herself to marrying him, she ought to trust him.

"Okay.'' She lifted her travel bag and headed for the bedroom, her heart in her throat. Back in the living room, she thought she heard Tyler humming, then the clink of glasses. Her stomach flip-flopped. What had she let herself in for?

The spacious room where Tyler slept was a monotone sand hue, from walls to vertical blinds to bedspread and carpet. Not a speck of color anywhere. Thankfully, Julie saw no signs of past lovers—no photos, mementos, tender love notes. If he'd kept a woman's picture on his bedside table, she didn't know what she'd have done. She shook off the unwelcome wave of possessiveness and dropped her bag on the bed.

She'd brought only what she could cram into the small canvas satchel. Her nightgown was a simple white flannel sacque with pink flowers, warm enough for cool March nights. Even though it was very conservative, she knew she'd feel vulnerable wearing it into the living room. Besides, she wanted to look appealing to Tyler, not frumpish.

Julie chose the cream-colored cotton leggings she wore when lounging about her apartment on weekends, and a turquoise sweater that hung comfortably off the curve of her shoulders and dropped below her hips. It was modest in design but a pretty robin's-egg shade that, she thought, brought out blue-green lights in her changeable eyes.

She opted for bare feet. Might as well start to get comfortable. After quickly brushing her hair, she sprayed a little perfume in the hollow of her throat and at both wrists, then applied a pale pink lip gloss. Taking a fortifying breath, she stepped out into the living room.

The fire was blazing. Tyler stood in the middle of the room watching the bedroom door as if he'd been waiting for her. He held out a crystal stem of bubbling golden stuff. The glass looked so fragile between his strong fingers, she wondered that it didn't shatter.

"That looks suspiciously like champagne." She accepted the glass cautiously.

"I decided the occasion deserved it."

"A fire and cuddling merit champagne? What do you serve when a lady agrees to spend the night?" She felt just a little evil, taunting him, but was gratified by a slow smile.

"I guess we'll just have to wait and see."

His gray eyes darkened, and she sensed how helpless a

prairie rabbit might feel under the gaze of a hungry wolf. But a second later, he smiled, the predator gone.

She lowered herself slowly to the edge of the couch. Tyler settled beside her, very close beside her. Reminded of how cozily his parents had sat in their own home, she took comfort that Tyler was just duplicating behavior patterns his family would expect from a married couple.

"The fire is lovely," she whispered, watching tongues of orange and gold dance and flicker. The logs crackled, popped, hissed pleasantly. As she took a sip of champagne and focused on the fire, she felt a few ounces of tension drain away.

"As a boy I used to experiment with matches," Tyler confessed. "I was fascinated by fire, but it was the mechanics of it that intrigued me, not its potential for destructiveness."

"You lit fires just to watch them burn?" Hadn't she read somewhere that little boys who literally played with fire often grew up to be violent men?

"Yeah, I loved studying them, experimenting with different materials to discover which burned the fastest, or not at all. I suppose I had some vague idea about fire-safe construction materials even then."

"But something made you stop," she guessed.

"Oh yeah. One day my dad caught me in the backyard. I knew what I was doing, always kept a hose nearby and wet down the ground around my experiments. But Dad was furious, wouldn't listen to explanations."

"You were punished?"

"Damn right. No TV for a month!"

"You must have been upset when he wouldn't hear you out." She sipped her champagne, enjoying the pictures in her mind of Tyler as a boy, already dreaming of the buildings he would someday erect.

He nodded. "Didn't mind not being able to watch my favorite shows. But I was hurt he didn't trust me to never endanger my family."

Julie was strangely moved by his story. Trust was important to him. It was a virtue she believed in and admired, too.

As Tyler spoke, he maneuvered his arm behind her shoulders. She didn't object to the harmless gesture. But when his wide hand curled gently inward, pulling her still closer, his fingers felt hot against the cool skin of her bare shoulder where the sweater had dropped low. When she looked up to try to read his expression, he was gazing down at her thoughtfully. He leaned forward to place his untouched champagne on the coffee table.

"I'm going to kiss you now," he said.

It was as if he understood she needed to prepare herself. "Yes," she said, "I know."

Tyler slowly lowered his head until their lips met. This time when they kissed, he started so softly she hardly felt any pressure. But a lovely glow penetrated her, spreading from her lips, along her jaw, and down her throat until her breasts felt flushed and full.

Tyler gently moved the tip of his tongue between her lips. She let him open her mouth, felt the pressure and warmth increase. Only when she began to return his kiss with a soft, eager groan did he press her back into the cushions and plunge deeply between her lips.

Her hand trembled violently. A drop of tingling, cold liquid hit the back of her wrist. It seemed it should evaporate into steam, her flesh felt so hot. As if Tyler knew she was about to drop her glass, he removed it from her fingertips and set it down beside his.

"Do you honestly think this will help me relax?" she asked skeptically. If anything, she felt more tightly strung.

"Definitely. Give yourself time." His hand came up and he lazily drew the lightly callused pads of his fingertips down her throat. She shivered, enjoying the contrast of roughness and tenderness. He dropped a kiss in the V of her sweater, then lower between her breasts. "Now isn't the time to be bashful about letting a man know what you want, Julie. Tell me to stop if you don't like what I'm doing."

But she felt incapable of communicating a single logical thought. She wasn't sure what she wanted or didn't want. She could only let him touch her, then react to each new feeling.

And, at the moment, her body seemed to be reacting in very pleasant ways. Curls of heat and little zings of electricity moved along mysterious paths through her torso. Corners of her body that had gone unnoticed all of her years seemed to burst to life, even though she wasn't *supposed* to feel anything for Tyler Fortune.

When the time for making her baby arrived, she had expected to have quick, mechanical intercourse with the man she married. She hadn't foreseen him being so charming, so gentle, so gosh-darn *good* at touching and kissing. Good enough to stir her up inside this way and strike matches to places that had felt wintry-cold forever.

Most of all, she hadn't expected Tyler to want to be with her in this way. An occasional, necessary intimacy would be the price he'd agree to pay to secure the wife he so desperately needed for business motives. Amazingly, he seemed to be putting a lot of energy into making her feel wanted. He actually seemed to be enjoying himself.

It's all a clever, clever act, she thought, letting herself drift. Lost to the moment, lost to his magical hands and wandering lips.

"Julie? Are you all right?"

Perhaps, she thought through a shimmering haze, this isn't the first time he's asked that question. His words barely intruded upon the music rising in her soul.

"My," she murmured, "that feels very…n-i-i-ice."

At some moment she couldn't define, his hand cupped her breast outside of her sweater. Then he was moving his palm in light circles over and around her heart. She wanted to curl up and weep for joy. She lifted her arm and let it fall limply across the back of his strong, muscled shoulders. His neck was so wide that her hand, from heel to fingertips, barely spanned it.

Arching her back, she pressed up against his palm. His lips trailed down her throat again then rested against the soft, blue wool over her breast, as if he was waiting for a sign from her.

Julie didn't want to think about the moment ending. She only knew she ached for more of his passion…or his flawless performance, if he, in fact, was just acting. This was an unexpected glimpse of heaven.

"Tell me now, Julie. What would you like me to do?" he whispered huskily in her ear. "I can stop now."

"No!" The word erupted from her lips as her eyes flew open. "Please don't stop." But how could she tell him what to do when she didn't have a blessed clue of the possibilities? She tried to remember romantic scenes in favorite movies. But all she could see were Tyler's gray eyes, beckoning to her, tempting her.

She felt as if she were being stalked, yet protected, too, as impossible as that seemed.

"Willing to take potluck, are you?" he growled from low in his throat.

She quivered at the cryptic promise in his words. She couldn't speak.

Easing her forward of the cushions, he lifted her sweater

up and over her head in one swift motion. Cool air hit her skin. Her immediate impulse was to cover herself with her arms, but she stopped herself in time. Pinning her arms stiffly to her sides she lifted her chin and allowed him to scrutinize her. He touched the lace cup of her bra, ran a finger along its upper edge. Then pulled it down until her nipple showed dark and rosy against the creamy lace.

"Beautiful," he whispered.

Julie squeezed her eyes shut, unable to watch any longer. The Earth spun, deliciously confusing, out of control, sliding off orbit into Saturn's rainbow rings. She felt incredibly torn between wanting to run from the room in utter embarrassment and aching to clutch Tyler to her and never release him. His hot breath crossed her breast. His mouth closed over one taut nipple. A tongue of agonizing, glorious fire angled down through her as his teeth rasped gently over the raised tip, reducing her to glowing ashes. He tormented her with his lips, his tongue, coaxing her toward ecstasy.

Arching higher, she grasped handfuls of his hair and pressed him harder to her. Not...what...I...expected! she thought wildly. Not this lust that wasn't just Tyler's...it was equally *hers*. And she hadn't even known it existed. She was breathing hard, taking in air in short fat gulps, thriving and dying from his caresses in the same second.

Julie heard herself cry out then buried a second, sharper shriek in the soft dark hair on top of his head that smelled of pine and leather and hot sand. After a moment, she realized Tyler had stopped moving. He was breathing hard; his lips had fallen open. His head rested between her breasts—one still covered by her bra, the other exposed and throbbing. She looked down, needing to know his thoughts. His eyes were wide, surprised.

"Tyler?" she whispered. "I'm sorry. I've done something wrong already?"

"Good grief," he moaned.

"I didn't mean to scream like that."

Tyler pushed off from her and after a quick, wistful glance at her breasts, pulled her sweater back into place, covering her. He felt as if he'd been mowed down by one of his own cement trucks. "You didn't do anything wrong. Don't apologize. You…" He struggled with words. "I just don't think you're ready for anything more, not yet."

The truth was, Tyler told himself, *he* was the one who wasn't ready. He hadn't been prepared for his bashful betrothed to take off like a rocket when they'd started necking. It had begun as a game for him. He'd been curious about how far she'd let him go before she put her foot down. But her dainty little toes had never hit the carpet!

Worse yet, he hadn't expected his own potent reaction to her, on levels he'd never experienced. He'd pegged Julie for one degree above frigid, told himself it would take him weeks of gentle cajoling, sweet-talking and dedicated effort to get her to spread those sweet librarian's legs. But he'd been wrong. She'd given him absolutely free rein, and he'd very nearly lost control in the storm of his own lust. He was pretty sure the two cries that had escaped her lips indicated she'd enjoyed an early climax. And all he'd done was play with her breasts.

The moment he'd started touching and kissing her—at first in the studied manner he'd applied to other women—he'd known she was different. Julie wasn't simply experiencing a physical reaction to a man's best attempts to get her into bed. She was naturally and innocently passionate in a way he'd never known a woman to be. If he was any judge at all of the female creature, Julie was a virgin. Yet she was as ripe as an August berry, ready to burst with succulent flavor. If he'd given in to his raging hormones, he'd have ripped off her clothes and been inside her before either of them could blink.

But it hadn't felt right. He was a savage, taking advantage of her inexperience. What had he gotten himself into?

The hell of it was, he actually *felt* something for this woman he intended to marry. Emotions were the worst possible complication for any business arrangement. And this unfamiliar mixture of guilt and yearning to cherish the woman in his arms was a dangerous way to feel toward a business partner.

With deep remorse on behalf of the fully aroused portion of his anatomy, Tyler slid away from Julie on the couch. It took another few moments to slow his pounding heart and gather the willpower to leave her. He stood up.

"That was a mistake," he said huskily. Coherent thought was impossible at the moment. He couldn't imagine the appropriate words to say to her. Striding across the room as fast as his rubbery legs would carry him, he hoped these would do as an apology.

Tyler stood in the middle of his kitchen for five…ten minutes…possibly longer, staring at the ice-and-water dispenser in the door of his refrigerator. Trying to catch his breath, trying to make sense of the last few minutes. He wondered if the soft sounds he heard coming from the other room were Julie's muffled sobs. He was too afraid to look.

Before he found the courage to step back into the living room and face the damage he had done, Julie appeared in the doorway, her eyes dry but suspiciously tinged with pink. She avoided his worried gaze, crossed the kitchen and turned on the burner under the kettle.

"I'm going to make myself a cup of tea, if you have any bags," she said succinctly.

"Everything got away from me," he murmured. "I'm sorry."

She nodded. "Tea bags?"

He pointed to the cupboard to her right. "I could have hurt you." When she reached for the makings of her tea and still didn't reply, he cleared his throat, considered giving her a good shake to get her attention, but quickly dismissed the idea. He'd unnerved her enough for one night. "It's better this way. We'll wait. After the wedding, we'll make your baby, but—"

"But we won't make love," she whispered. "Not really."

He looked at her in disbelief. A few hours ago, he wouldn't have believed her sweet features could ever look hard. But Julie's lovely fawn eyes had turned steely and determined. Her half smile was brittle. The teakettle began to whistle.

He was confused now. "There are clinical means of impregnating a woman. But I thought you didn't want—"

"You can't *possibly* know what I want!" Julie rounded on him, hot teapot in one hand, her other balled into a tight little fist in front of her. She shook both at him.

"No," he said cautiously, "I guess not." He'd never learned how to deal with an angry woman. A quick kiss? A pat on the bottom? Flowers? His mother responded well to hugs. He figured he'd probably get christened with the teapot if he tried any of the above now. "Julie, tell me why you're so upset." He took the teapot from her and set it behind him on the countertop, out of range.

She looked directly at him, and he was sure her eyes had never been more appealing than right at that moment, snapping with anger. "I can't explain." She bit off her words.

"Maybe you're reacting to the situation, not to me," he

suggested hopefully. "This is all a little weird. We both know we're not in love with each other...and probably never will be. If you'd had lovers before, you'd know it's asking for trouble to pretend otherwise."

She tossed her head. There was fire in her eyes. "How do you know I haven't had tons of lovers before you?"

He made a valiant effort to stop himself from laughing. The best he could do was choke off the impulse under the guise of a cough. "I suppose I'm just guessing, since you told me you hadn't gone out on many dates. Sorry if I presumed—"

"Well, I should hope so."

He stared at her. Where was this coming from—this hidden spunkiness?

"I was just looking out for your best interests," he tried to explain.

"You don't know me. How can you tell me what's best for me?"

"All right. Fair enough." He decided he needed tea now as much as she, if not something a good deal stronger. Quickly, he took out two mugs, dropped a tea bag in each and sloshed as much water as possible over them from the kettle. Before the tea finished brewing, he took three rapid swallows of the weak but boiling-hot liquid. He put the mug down with a thump. "Enough of the guessing games," he said firmly. "You're going to tell me what you want...now."

The demand seemed to startle her. She blinked up at him, and he could almost see the question turning over and over in her mind, like a pebble tumbling downhill. *What do I want? What do I want?*

It was fascinating, watching her features soften, her eyes grow distant with concentration, her lips press together in thought. It struck him in this dim light that, when she was preoccupied with other things and not concerned with her nervous habits, she was quite lovely.

"Do you want me to make love to you?"

A flash of panic crossed her eyes. "I—well…" Unexpectedly, she let out a nervous laugh. "How do they put it? I believe the moment has passed?"

Unfortunately, it hadn't passed for him. He had wanted her when he had her pinned to his couch and she was melting in his arms. And he wanted her now, even though her usual charming air of helplessness had been replaced by a tentative streak of will. She might have been offended by the way he'd kissed her and fondled her…but he still wanted her. And what maddened him more than anything was…he knew he'd still want her just as badly even if she felt nothing for him.

"I guess it has," he lied. But he couldn't help hoping it would return. If not in the morning, then some time the next day…or the next…or, at least, soon. He was praying for very soon.

This is a turning point in my life. The thought came to Julie in a flash of insight at three o'clock the next morning, as she lay awake in Tyler Fortune's bed, staring at Tyler Fortune's condo ceiling, remembering the feeling of Tyler Fortune's lips against hers.

Julie knew deep within her soul that what had happened the night before, and whatever she decided to do this morning, would determine her future. It was as if a power beyond her imagination had reached down from the heavens, swept her up off the dusty streets of Houston and dropped her down here in Pueblo, Arizona. Which might as well be called Fortuneville for all the power Tyler's family wielded in this town. And now that she was here, she was being forced to choose between two totally different lives. The most troublesome thing was, she wanted and feared both of her options for different reasons.

Julie tossed on the bed, feeling that if by some chance she could find a comfortable position she might also discover a solution to her dilemma. What were her choices? Return to her safe, humble life, numb to the world, avoiding contact with strangers. Alone. It wasn't a bad life. But she couldn't honestly say she'd ever be happy in it.

Or she could keep her word and take one terrifyingly brave leap into the world of the Fortune family. It would be the most dangerous thing she'd ever done. She'd been waiting a lifetime to love and be loved, and children were a guarantee of that love.

Men were different, she thought in frustration, thrusting her hands beneath her head. Men were incapable of love…at least, not the sort women experienced. They pretended sincerity and devotion to get what they wanted. Just as Tyler had pretended his passion for her the night before, because he'd been in the mood for sex. And she'd been convenient.

She didn't blame him. He was just doing what came naturally to the male of any species. But for just the briefest of times she'd lost herself in the fantasy he'd woven around them. And that had made his walking away from her, after he'd made her need him, all the more painful.

She wouldn't let that happen again. If she really did stay in Pueblo and he came to her another night, she would give him her body because that was part of their deal. But she wouldn't surrender her heart.

With the first light of day, Julie leaned over the side of the king-size bed where she'd slept alone and reached down to the floor for her overnight bag. She pulled out a denim skirt and pink oxford shirt, underclothes and panty hose, and took them into the adjoining bathroom. When she finished showering and washing her hair, she used two of the thick white towels stored under the sink to dry off, then blew-dry her hair.

From the other room, she heard the telephone ring. It took Tyler four rings to answer it. *He* was obviously sleeping as soundly as a baby—unaffected by last night's drama.

A moment later, as she was applying a thin sweep of pale peach lip gloss, he knocked on her door. ''Come in,'' she said coolly.

He cracked the door but didn't step inside, and she was struck by the odd expression on his face—something close to sheepishness. ''It's my grandmother. She wants to know if noon is okay to go shopping.''

Her wedding gown! Once she let Kate buy her a gown, there would be no turning back. Go…or stay? She must decide now. Return to safe dreariness, or step off an emotional cliff and plunge headlong into a colorful but terrifying family? ''Noon is fine,'' she whispered.

Five

"**I** know I said this last night, but it bears repeating. I'm so very glad our Tyler found you, my dear. I've been so worried about him," Kate said as she pulled her sleek silver Mercedes convertible into a parking space close to one of the entrances to the fashionable mall at Saguaro Valley.

Julie could only wonder what this proud, gracious woman would think of her if she knew the truth. She felt utterly undeserving of this extravagant shopping trip.

"Thank you," Julie said, "I hope I'll live up to your expectations."

Kate smiled, her pale eyes twinkling with pleasure. "Oh, you will, you will. Now, let's go have some fun." As they walked through the elegant etched-glass doors into the art nouveau mall, Kate reached for Julie's hand. "Let me have another look at this diamond."

Julie smiled and offered her left hand. It was a beautiful

ring. Two perfect carats, the round solitaire set in a gold eight-pronged mounting with no adornments to distract from its blue-white fire.

"Do you like it, my dear?" Kate asked.

"Oh, yes," she said. "I told Tyler when we went into the jeweler's I didn't want anything too busy. No side stones or fancy modern designs. Just a simple solitaire. I would have been happy with just one carat, but he said you'd send him back if he came home with less than two."

Kate roared with laughter. "The boy knows his grandmother!"

Although Kate encouraged Julie to try on as many gowns as she liked, Julie's eye immediately settled on a simple dress of heavy, buttery satin without lace, sequins or pearls. A boat neckline scooped modestly below her throat and over her narrow shoulders. The three-quarter-length sleeves were fitted snugly around her lower arms with tiny satin-covered buttons. She'd never worn anything with covered buttons. They seemed such an elegant touch. The bodice was tapered so close to her own shape it felt like a luxurious second skin, and the skirt fell wide in front of her toes, then lengthened in the back to flow into a short train. Aware of who Julie was marrying, the saleswoman pressed her to try gowns encrusted with glittering layers of hand-appliquéd lace, crystal beads and baby pearls. Kate also attempted to interest her in more elaborate gowns. But Julie politely turned them all down. This was *her* gown.

"It suits you," Kate approved at last, "just as your ring does. On your wedding day, you should wear only what makes you happy."

The veil was chosen as quickly. Few alterations were necessary, only an inch off the gown's hem. But when Kate informed the boutique's owner she would personally pick up the gown in two days, the woman looked shocked.

Julie cracked a smile as they left the shop. "Such a hurried wedding…she must be suspicious and just bursting with gossip."

"I'm sure she is. Pueblo has a small-town mentality and is very conservative, for all its fine stores and new construction. Everyone knows everyone else's business here— and you snuck up on them, my dear. Within a few hours they'll all know the wedding date, where the ceremony will be, the name of the caterer, and how many will be in the bridal party."

Julie frowned. "The church. That's the real problem, isn't it?"

"Taken care of already," Kate assured her with a wave of her hand and a toss of her silver head, "although the outcome is different than I'd originally planned."

"How is that?"

"Oh, I had brunch this morning with the pastor. He couldn't make room in his schedule without bumping another couple. So I've decided you'll be married in the garden at the ranch."

"That would be lovely," Julie agreed.

"I also lined up the caterer for the reception and gave Adele the job of booking the photographer and a string quartet."

Julie shook her head in amazement and swallowed over a growing lump in her throat as they walked through the mall bustling with shoppers. "You're going to so much trouble. This must all seem so strange to you, the way Tyler and I are rushing this marriage."

Kate chuckled. "Oh, don't apologize, my dear. Tyler has never done anything the easy way. He has a mind of his own. When he decides he wants something, he goes after it, and, more often than not, gets it. You, apparently, are what he wants…and he's not willing to wait." She smiled delightedly. "I think it's rather romantic, myself. Being desired that fiercely by a man. It's no small thing." Kate winked at her. "But you must know that."

He doesn't desire or love me, she wanted to say. *This is all a farce. Don't be taken in.* But the warning was as true for herself as it was for Kate. If she wasn't careful, she'd end up believing the fantasy. And what then? If she ever came to her senses, the pain would kill her.

With the gown chosen and all other details under control, Kate whisked Julie off to a light lunch, then to a spa located at one end of the mall. Here Julie was treated to a makeover under Kate's personal direction. She gave up trying to convince Kate she didn't want anything drastic done to alter her appearance. The woman was on a mission; she was not to be deterred.

Kate consulted with the hairstylist, colorist, manicurist and massage therapist. Then they all went to work as a team. By the end of the afternoon, Julie had been trimmed, tinted, buffed, toned and wrapped in a blue silk dress Kate had plucked from the adjoining boutique while Julie was trapped in the stylist's chair.

"I don't feel like myself," she sighed as they left the shop to the approving oohs and ahs of the staff. "I'm a fraud in fancy duds and someone else's hair."

"Don't be silly," Kate said. "You're simply making the most of what you have, and the effect is charming. Utterly charming, my dear."

"Do you think Tyler will…will like me like this?" she breathed.

Kate picked up her pace. "Do *you* like the way you look?"

"Well, I—I really don't know," she stammered. "It will take some…yes, I guess I do."

"Then what Tyler thinks is of little importance. He

loves you and he'll learn to appreciate the things you do to make yourself feel and look attractive.''

Julie's stomach sank. If Tyler's reaction depended upon his loving her, she was lost. As surely as she knew the difference between Chaucer and Shakespeare, she understood that Tyler's feelings for her didn't even approach love.

What in the blazes, Tyler wondered as he watched a young woman climb out of Kate's car, had Kate done with his prim fiancée? The anger subsided as he observed the slim beauty pulling shopping bags out of the car.

Tyler had worked all afternoon at corporate headquarters, but he'd found it difficult to concentrate on any one task. He'd imagined Julie being dragged from store to store by whirlwind Kate, then dropped off at the condo by mid-afternoon to fend for herself. He'd told himself he should at least check on her, maybe take her for a drive across the desert to fill her time. But when he'd arrived at the condo, there was no sign of Julie. He'd been ready to start driving around town to look for them, when Kate's car had pulled up.

Although he couldn't put his finger on exactly what changes had been woven by his grandmother's spell, he decided they were generally pleasing changes. Just enough to enhance Julie's best features. Her hair was trimmed and styled in a slightly shorter coiffure that framed her face in a smoothly glistening cap of chestnut-brown, slightly redder than its natural shade.

Her makeup was the most clever of all. It wasn't overdone or garish. A pale shade of taupe eye shadow and liner only highlighted her eyes. Coral lipstick accentuated her full mouth. A sweep of color and shading brought out cheekbones. She even seemed to have acquired a subtly provocative lilt to her walk as she juggled bags and followed Kate up the walk, smiling and laughing at something his grandmother had just said.

It was only when she started up the steps and shifted back into her customary hesitant gait that he was reminded of the painfully awkward young woman he'd taken to dinner. Underneath, she was still just as insecure as before. He relaxed. She wasn't a threat.

She was still…just Julie. Julie with lipstick and a new dress. This he could deal with.

"Good evening, ladies," he crowed when they walked through the door and into the living room. "Need any help with packages?"

"Tyler dear, I'm so glad you're here." Kate strode across the room with remarkable energy for an octogenarian. She dropped four fat shopping bags on the floor beside the couch, then lowered herself into its tan leather cushions. "I'll take a glass of white wine, please. What an afternoon! Julie? Wine, dear?"

"I don't usually—" She glanced up at Tyler.

He grinned at her. "If you don't have any, my dear sweet grandmother may feel obligated to finish off the entire bottle herself."

"Well then," Julie said with a smile, "I guess I should help out."

After he'd poured them each a glass of wine and himself a scotch, he settled into his favorite armchair to be a proper audience to their adventures. As Kate babbled on and pulled items from bags, Tyler studied the new Julie with interest. She seemed more animated than he remembered her. Her face brightened, softened, then puckered in concentration as Kate described their shopping triumphs. He found himself enjoying the childish delight Julie seemed to take in a simple gals' day out, and he wondered if she'd ever allowed herself such a treat. Most likely, she'd never been able to afford a no-holds-barred assault on an upscale shopping mall.

When Kate at last declared herself exhausted and took her leave, Julie stood at the living-room window, her wineglass delicately balanced between her fingertips, watching the older woman drive off with a look of regret in her soft eyes.

Tyler was touched. One minute Julie was a lovely grown woman, the next she was a child watching her playmate leave, needing reassurance there would be other days as joyful. Stepping up behind her, he gently wrapped his arms around her waist. "She likes you a lot."

"We had such…such *fun!*" she said with a note of amazement in her voice.

He laughed. "My grandmother is tons of fun. But she can also be a heap of trouble when her plans don't coincide with yours."

"I think all of her ideas are wonderful." Julie sighed then turned her head to look up at him over her shoulder. "Except maybe for the gown."

"You two argued about the wedding dress?"

"Oh, no," she said quickly. "I just had a different opinion of what I should wear."

"And are you very disappointed with what Kate chose for you?"

Julie grinned smugly at him. "I didn't say I gave in."

He was shocked. "You ended up with the gown *you* picked out?"

"I knew what I wanted, and Kate agreed that it suited me."

He shook his head. "That's a first. She can be as stubborn as a—"

"She's lovely," Julie cut him off. Another first, he thought. "I had a wonderful day with her."

He found himself touching his lips to her hair, inhaling the fragrance of the salon's shampoo. Strawberries, he thought. Then his attention dropped lower. Her bottom was pressing into the muscled front of his thighs. She shifted slightly within his arms as if she too was aware of the intimacy of their position. She stood silently within the circle of his arms. He told himself to release her, but couldn't. They watched the sun set behind the mountains. Purple streaks against rose. Her body grew warmer against his.

"What are we doing?" she whispered at last.

"I don't know about you, but I'm…thinking."

"About what?"

"You," he said. And wasn't it true? He'd been pondering many things that concerned her all day long. Like how much he still wanted her. And how vividly he remembered last night. Sitting at his desk, he'd imagined the velvet-soft curve of her breast under his palm. He saw her nipple harden and peak. In his heated mind he'd devoured her again.

"About my new haircut?" she asked innocently. Was there a shadow of playfulness in her tone?

"No. Just…well, about different things. I came home at three o'clock, assuming you would be back from shopping and might be lonely."

"Ah," she said. He wished he could see her expression but she'd turned her face away.

"I guess I didn't need to worry."

"I've been on my own a long time, Tyler." She seemed to relax another notch in his arms. Her head rested against his chest. She was a good foot shorter than he. Although he'd always been attracted to statuesque women, he liked the way the curves of Julie's body tucked neatly into the muscled hollows of his own. "I'm used to finding ways to fill my time."

"I suppose so." Suddenly he wanted to be the one to fill her time, at least this corner of it. "What do you want to do for dinner?"

"I don't know. I'll make something for us, if you like."

"That's right, you enjoy gourmet cooking. And I enjoy eating. I wouldn't mind taking you out, though."

"I'd rather stay in tonight." Her voice sounded a little breathless. "If it's all the same to you. You know, get used to the kitchen," she added quickly.

"Of course."

"Tyler?"

"Yes."

"I can't cook if you don't let go of me."

"Oh." He quickly released her but felt disappointed when she easily moved out of his arms leaving an empty, cool space down his front. He turned away quickly, a silent curse stopping at his lips, hoping she wouldn't notice the telltale ridge beneath his jeans' zipper.

Suddenly he felt shy around her—a new sensation for him. Women had never made him feel awkward before, maybe because he'd always felt in control. The more he saw of Julie, the less in control he felt.

"Let me see what you have in the fridge for ingredients," she said brightly, practically skipping out of the room in her enthusiasm.

He stood where he'd been, facing the window and looking out at the darkening horizon. But his mind was no longer on the rouged skyline of Pueblo. Every one of his senses was tuned to the woman banging around happily in his kitchen. He knew exactly where she was by the sound of her footsteps across the tile—moving around the breakfast bar, opening and closing the squeaky pantry door, heading for the refrigerator. The refrigerator door wheezed open. She would be standing in front of it now, tapping one toe while picking out promising ingredients. He could almost see the frown on her pretty face as she studied with disapproval its sparse contents. The door shut.

"Well, you do have a sirloin steak in the freezer!" she called out. "And a few potatoes in the pantry. If you don't mind canned veggies, I think we can have a fairly acceptable meal."

"I don't want to put you to any trouble," he said quickly, although steak, spuds and a quiet evening in his own home without having to put on a show for a date sounded incredibly appealing.

"Cooking for two is no more trouble than cooking for one," she pronounced cheerfully. "I don't eat beef very often, but if I do I like to splurge on a really good cut of meat. This baby looks scrumptious."

"Then steak it is," he said, crossing the living room to the kitchen doorway. He watched her take the frozen packet from the freezer, unwrap the meat, place it on a plate then slide it into the microwave. "You're not going to nuke it, are you?" he asked in horror.

"No, silly. I'm just defrosting it."

"Oh." Leaning against the doorjamb, he let his glance follow her as she moved around his kitchen, searching out what she needed, shaking her head occasionally at something that seemed to bother her about his limited collection of seasonings. He found it impossible to take his eyes off her. Whereas she was ill at ease around strangers and in public places, here, in his kitchen, she was mistress of her domain.

Within a few minutes she'd located a bottle of cider vinegar, some hard lumps of brown sugar, powdered ginger, garlic powder and tamari soy sauce. She blended them into an aromatic marinade with which she doused the steak. He wanted to tell her she was ruining a perfectly good piece of meat, but held back, curious to see how it would turn out.

When the meal was ready, they brought their plates to the small golden-oak table at one end of the kitchen. He lit a candle and placed it between them. Julie's eyes glowed when he dimmed the electric light overhead. He sat down across from her.

"Sure looks good," he said, speaking of more than the food.

She grinned back at him and cut a nibble from one corner of her portion of steak. When she chewed, she closed her eyes and savored it. Tyler ached to lick the juice from her lips.

It seemed remarkable to him that he actually was able to taste the meal. As good as it was, his attention was held by Julie, not the food. She was a wizard with a plain hunk of beef! When she at last placed her fork and knife across her plate and pushed back her chair to stand, he stopped her with a hand over hers.

"Sit still and finish your wine. You cooked; I'll clean up."

"But you don't need—"

"Fair is fair," he said firmly. "This is a partnership, remember?"

Julie studied Tyler's expression for a moment, then sank back down into her chair thoughtfully. "Yes," she said softly, "I remember."

It had seemed to her that this dinner was the most romantic she'd ever shared with a man. Even better than the night at Van Gogh's. Yet it was equally clear from Tyler's silence during the meal that he was untouched by romantic thoughts, at least when it came to her. With a shudder she drew her hand from beneath his and obediently sipped the last of her wine.

"Why don't you unpack your things," he suggested as he rinsed their plates and put them into the dishwasher. "Get comfortable for the night."

She mechanically pushed herself up from her chair and walked back to the bedroom. Well, she thought, at least he seemed to like my cooking. He'd devoured the marinated steak and oven-roasted potatoes as if he hadn't eaten in a week.

She found hangers in the walk-in closet and made space for her new outfits along the far right side, so as not to crowd Tyler's clothing. Reaching out, she touched a neatly pressed white dress shirt. Silk, she thought, making a mental note for the future. No starch. All of his clothing, even the things he wore to work in, looked expensive. Except for the exquisite items Kate had bought for her, all of her own clothing was practical, well-worn, out of fashion.

"What are you doing now?" Tyler's voice asked from the bedroom doorway.

"Hanging up my new duds," she said without turning around. Julie ran her hand down the sleeve of a peach-colored sweater dress Kate had insisted they buy. It was the color of ripe fruit. Angora blended with wool and silk. It had felt like heaven when she tried it on.

"Do you like them?" he asked from closer behind her.

"Oh, yes." She nearly purred with pleasure. "Your grandmother has such wonderful taste."

"Model your favorite for me."

"What?" She couldn't help laughing as she spun around.

"Change into the outfit you like the best. Show me how

it looks on you," he insisted. His eyes challenged her; one corner of his lips twisted upward provocatively.

She felt as if she'd walked into a blast furnace. "Well, I suppose that would be the teal cocktail dress," she said tentatively. "But you'll see it soon enough. Your grandmother said I should wear it to the reception she's giving so that I can meet the rest of the family."

"I'd rather see it now." He backed off and lowered himself onto the bed. A mischievous gleam flickered beneath the surface of his gray eyes, worrying her. One second he looked boyishly playful, the next he was the Papago brave, stalking his prey.

He's just a man, no different from anyone else, she told herself.

Sweeping the hanger with the blue-green sequined dress off the closet pole, she headed for the bathroom. Just as she reached for the knob, Tyler cleared his throat loudly.

"What is it now?" she asked with a touch of exasperation.

"Don't you think hiding in the bathroom to change your clothing is unnecessary?"

Julie scowled at him. "What are you talking about?"

"After all, I'm going to be seeing quite a lot of that pretty body of yours."

"My body isn't pretty," she snapped.

Julie was shocked that she'd said it. She'd revealed far too much of herself in that one brief sentence. The expression on Tyler's face shifted from eager playfulness to puzzlement. He stretched out long and lean on the bed, his boots propped on the foot rail, hands wedged beneath his head, observing her.

"How did you ever arrive at that?"

She shrugged, prickling under his scrutiny. "I know my own strengths and weaknesses. I'm a good cook. I'm a hard worker. But I'm no fashion model. I don't have a tiny waist, long legs or big…well, you know.'' She was sure her cheeks couldn't possibly get any redder.

"Perhaps," he allowed, without saying whether or not he agreed, "but my guess is—whatever you're hiding under those prissy garments is more than adequate to any man's needs. I've already witnessed two of your lovely assets." His gaze moved meaningfully toward her chest as he pushed himself off the bed again. He was so quick she didn't have time to react before he'd crossed the room and swept her into his arms.

The dress fell from her startled hand to the floor. "Wh-what are you doing?"

He pretended not to hear her question. "I don't have to see you naked, Julie Parker, to imagine your shape or know how it would be to make love to you. I can feel your body through your clothes even now. You have a very nice shape." He pressed her to him, touching his lips to the side of her neck. "A damn nice shape. And I know from earlier experience, a man could happily enjoy your sweet breasts for a very long time."

Trembling, she dropped her forehead against his chest and squeezed her eyes tightly shut. "Please don't patronize me."

"I don't say things I don't mean, Julie. You claim you want babies, not sex. But why not relax and enjoy the process of getting pregnant? You aren't afraid of me anymore, are you?"

"Of course not, I—well, not you so much as—" How could she explain? She hardly understood her own reluctance to get close to a man. Any man.

"I won't hurt you," he murmured. "And I know I said we should wait. But I want you something wicked, woman.

If someone harmed you in the past, I'm sorry. But that man isn't me. Do you understand?''

She nodded slowly, then dared to look up at him.

As Tyler watched her eyes dilate and fill with emotion at his touch, his heart went out to her. "I'll take it slow," he promised. "You tell me if I do anything that frightens you or that you don't enjoy. Agreed?''

"Yes," she breathed weakly.

He wondered—was it coincidence or by design that his relationships had always been with women who didn't require trust, but casually accepted propositions from men of wealth or pleasing physiques? Maybe it had been a comfort to him, knowing they'd easily move on to their next affair after he was out of their lives. They never threatened his freedom, and he never felt sorry for them when he stopped calling because he was certain they wouldn't miss him.

But now, holding this fragile creature called Julie, he asked himself if that sort of shallow, selfish relationship would ever be enough for him again. He wanted to comfort, caress, make love to her slowly, taking days…weeks if necessary to teach her the ultimate joys of being loved by a man. Moreover, he believed in the depths of his soul that he was the only man for the job. Why that was, he had no idea. He only sensed that she wanted him to show her the way.

But he also was sharply aware of the delicacy of her emotional state. So many changes were rushing into her life—new people, a different place to live, an unfamiliar lifestyle. He would have to take her mind off all that, then give her only another taste of the sexual awakening awaiting her. Just as much as she could handle at one time.

The problem was, he didn't know if he could measure himself out that way. He wanted every inch of her…*now!*

He was starving for her. The gentle kisses of a new lover and long moments spent dreaming in each other's arms weren't going to satisfy his own ravenous hunger.

"Forget about the dress for now," he said tightly, brushing his lips against her softly mussed hair. "Come over here with me. Let's talk."

She lifted her head from his shirt front as he turned her toward the bed. "You want to do it now, don't you?" she whispered, so faintly he could barely hear her.

His smile was tight. "I would like very much to make love to you," he admitted. The next part was hard as hell. "But I won't."

She looked up at him, crushed. "Why not?"

"Because you're not ready."

"I'm marrying you, aren't I?"

He chuckled, shaking his head. "Contrary to what I recently believed, one seems to have little to do with the other. At least in your case. Here," he said, patting the bed, "sit down."

She obeyed, but he could feel the trembling of her body through the mattress.

"Now tell me what I've done to terrify you so? Or is it all men who affect you this way?"

She took a deep breath, let it out, drew another. As though denying a secret terror, she moved her head slowly from side to side.

"A partnership of any kind requires communication." He took her hand in his and pulled it gently into his lap. "If we're going through with this marriage, each of us has to understand the other person's needs, fears, desires…the whole enchilada. If we go into this blindly, it just won't work."

"That makes perfect sense," she admitted after a moment's hesitation. "But I've never talked about…about *this sort of thing* with anyone, not even with another woman.''

He frowned. ''About sex?''

She shrugged helplessly, and he could tell how difficult this was for her. They were breaking down barriers that had controlled her entire life. She blinked away the beginnings of tears, but her eyes remained moist, troubled.

''I don't like thinking about some things. Like how strong a man is and how physically weak a woman is…at least someone like me…and how there's…well, there's just no way to stop him from—'' She'd been on a roll, but suddenly stopped as if she'd hit a wall.

''From what, Julie? From hurting you?''

She tilted her head to one side and looked up at him, almost accusingly. A sharp pain sliced through him. Damn the man who'd done this to her.

''Were you raped, Julie?''

''N-no,'' she stammered, squeezing his hand as if to reassure him. At least, it wasn't that. ''Not me, not…it wasn't like that. I just learned not to trust men because—'' She sniffled and wiped tears away with the back of her free hand. ''It was my first year of college. I hadn't dated much at all in high school, mostly because word got around among the boys that I wouldn't let them do the things they wanted to do to girls.'' She smiled wanly.

''Typical so far,'' he commented, giving her a reassuring hug. ''When adolescent male hormones flow, we can be a darn persistent sex. Go on.''

''The dorm I was assigned to in college was girls-only, but the boys' dorm was just across the quad. We took turns throwing parties. Most of the girls were no more experienced than I was, but they were ready for a little adventure. And dry parties just weren't cool.''

''So the beer ran freely,'' he guessed.

"Yes, and after some of the girls in my dorm got sloshed pretty thoroughly, the boys talked them…us…into playing a game. They turned out the lights in one room and one girl was sent into it. Then a boy went in and said something silly to her. She had to guess whose voice she heard even though he tried to disguise his voice. It was just a stupid game, really, and at first seemed so harmless."

"I see." He was pretty sure he knew where this so-called game was headed, but he let her tell her story. She had to relieve herself of past nightmares, and if this was what it took the time would be well spent.

"Well," she continued hesitantly, "then it became a kissing game. You know, she had to guess which of the boys was kissing her. Again, I didn't really see the harm in it, but when one of the boys decided I should identify something other than his lips, I got frightened and left."

In spite of her serious tone, Tyler chuckled. "I'm sorry, I know that must have shocked and terrified you. But I can just see some drunken college kid stumbling into a dark room and dropping trou."

Julie silenced him with a stern look, which softened when he shrugged apologetically.

"I guess my point is," he said, "you were using good sense when you took off."

She nodded solemnly. "The next morning, three of the girls from the party weren't in their rooms. They were in the infirmary. They'd been assaulted and raped. They were bruised and terribly injured, physically and emotionally. I was horrified by the violence and assumed the police would act quickly. But my friend Eleanor, one of those who'd been hurt, told me nothing was being done. The police claimed the girls had willingly entered into a sex game with the boys, and it was unlikely a case of rape could be supported."

Tyler wasn't shocked by her story; he'd heard of similar incidents and they sickened him, making him glad he'd never taken part in that sort of thing. Mostly, he was relieved to learn Julie hadn't been one of the unlucky three. "So no more parties for Julie?"

"Right," she said. "And I decided dating people I didn't know wasn't safe. The only problem was, I'm not a very outgoing person so even after I graduated and started working I didn't make a lot of friends."

"So you remained a virgin in search of a baby but not necessarily a man."

"Something like that," she agreed with a self-conscious laugh. "I tried rooming with a couple of other women, but they were forever trying to set me up with men. And their idea of great dates for me were guys I wouldn't share a ten-minute conversation with."

He thought for a moment. "All men aren't monsters, Julie. How about we take some time to get to know each other. When you're ready to take the next step, you tell me. Before the wedding or after. I promise I'll be patient."

For a long while she just looked at him, delving into his eyes as if searching for the hidden lie, the trick. But when she found nothing to alarm her, she smiled tentatively. "All right."

Grateful she'd agreed to at least let him try to get close to her, Tyler stretched out on his side and pulled a pillow down for himself, another for her. He patted hers, and, after a second's hesitation, she stiffly lay back on it and stared up at the ceiling. Clearly, he had a long way to go.

Julie tried, she really tried to let the muscles in her body unknot. She wanted to trust Tyler, but wanting something and actually feeling it were two different things when you were fighting a lifetime of habit. She closed her eyes and listened to him talk to her.

"The Amish have a practice called bundling." He spoke in a mellow voice, almost as if he were calming an anxious child. "The engaged couple sleep in the same bed, but remain clothed. I always imagined it might be a good way to begin to feel comfortable with another person—lying alone together on a soft bed, talking, sharing dreams, learning about fears, interests, hopes for the future without the pressure of sex."

"Are you suggesting we do that?" she asked warily.

"Would sharing this bed with me, fully clothed just as we are now, frighten you?"

"No," she admitted, giving him an appreciative smile, "I don't believe it would."

Six

Their first night, she wore her favorite oversize shirt and cozy leggings; he came to bed in loose-fitting sweats and was endearingly careful not to touch her at all. They lay on their backs at opposite edges of the mattress, staring up at the white ceiling, talking in whispers about whatever came to their minds. She told Tyler things in the dark she'd never spoken of to another living soul. Sweet confidences she'd barely allowed herself to think.

He confided in her, too. His torn feelings over his role in the Fortune clan. His fear that something might stop construction of the hospital—like the investigation into his foreman's death. He hated waiting in lines and loved dogs. He never hesitated to take on a physical challenge that carried him up a sheer cliff on ropes or down a black-diamond trail on skis, but he had an unreasoning fear of spiders. Tyler never said so, but Julie was sure no other women had heard these confessions from him.

Knowing he trusted her to keep his secrets was like stepping into a soothing shower of confidence. But inevitably the sadness returned, because there was an all-too-clear reason for his not spending hours sharing his deepest feelings with those other women. He'd been too busy making love to them. He obviously didn't find her as irresistible, and that hurt.

The third night she shared Tyler's bed felt like midsummer. It hadn't been hot enough to use the air conditioner during the day, and Julie had left the windows in the condo open to catch the rare breeze off the desert. Tyler exchanged his sweats for a clean T-shirt and boxers, but beads of sweat still clung to the small hairs at the back of his neck.

"You look so uncomfortable," she commented as they climbed onto opposite sides of the bed. "Maybe I should close up the house and turn on the air after all."

"It will cool down soon enough," he said. "Leave the windows open."

But she could feel heat radiating from his body, between the sheets, and soon she was too hot to sleep. "Let's be sensible about this," she murmured into the dark. "Before I came, what did you usually sleep in?"

"Nothing."

She could feel him grinning. Was he just trying to get a rise out of her? "How about a compromise? You can take off your shirt if you leave on your boxers."

"Thank God!" He dramatically tossed off the covers. She watched in the moonlight as he stripped off his T-shirt. She held her breath as he hesitated, his thumbs tucked into the waistband of his shorts as if considering dropping them to the floor as well.

"Don't you dare," she warned him.

He shrugged and gave her a sheepish look that said, *Can't blame a guy for trying.*

"Now you," he said, crawling back under the sheet.

Julie's mouth went dry. She tried to swallow but failed. "I'm fine as I am."

Suddenly, he rolled over on the bed, pressed his mouth to her cheek then flicked his tongue out. "Pretty salty for a woman who isn't sweating. Don't you have anything lighter than that monster shirt?"

"Not with me."

"Well, at least take off those long johns."

"They're not long johns," she corrected him primly. "They're leggings."

"Whatever. You need to cool down or you'll never get any sleep. Tomorrow's a big day. The rehearsal and dinner with the family."

She hadn't forgotten, and he was right. She desperately needed a good night's rest. Her days had been spent on the phone, notifying the library she wouldn't be working there any longer, letting her landlord know that she was moving and would come for her things after the wedding. Closing down one life so that she could begin another. The idea both frightened and excited her.

Julie turned her head on the silky percale pillowcase to look at Tyler. He was studying her, thinking his private thoughts behind those dark Papago eyes. She would have given anything to know what they were.

"At least take off the leggings," he repeated.

"I can't."

"Why?"

"I don't have anything on under them," she said reluctantly.

A flash of white teeth sent a shiver through her. "Now that's intriguing. But that shirt comes down to your knees. You'd be quite decent even if you removed the leg thingies."

She was too tired to argue with him. Reaching beneath the sheet, she tugged off the cotton leggings and dropped them onto the floor beside the bed. "Satisfied? Now we're both comfortable and can get some sleep. Good night, Tyler."

She lay very still, listening to his breathing. Why hadn't he answered her?

After a moment, his hand came across the mattress and she tensed. But his long fingers only folded around hers, softly, easily, companionably. This is nice, she thought. Holding hands in bed.

A moment later, his thumb moved up to her wrist and gently circled over her pulse point. Julie felt her body settle into itself. The last strands of tension eased away. She rolled onto her side, laid her palm against Tyler's strong jaw, and looked down into his eyes. He was waiting for her, holding his breath. She brushed her hand cautiously across his smooth, sun-bronzed cheek, over his wide forehead. She touched fingertips to his expressive lips. He didn't try to kiss them. He waited. Suddenly unsure of herself, she started to lower her hand and move away.

"Please don't stop," he whispered. "I've had a killer headache all day. That felt good."

How could she deny him such a simple kindness? "Is this where it hurts?" She gently trailed the backs of her fingers across his taut forehead, then smoothed the tense flesh around his eyes and across his temple.

"Wonderful," he murmured.

She kept her hand in motion, wishing him relief. When his own hand came up to rest, as if by chance, against her throat, she didn't flinch. She was considering how very nice this felt when Tyler turned his head barely an inch, caught her moving fingertips between his strong white teeth, and nibbled gently.

She looked down at him, transfixed by the intimacy of the gesture. She didn't pull away.

Slowly, his lips parted and he gently drew one of her fingers between his teeth. His tongue circled her fingertip in a warm, moist bath. She shivered and stared in fascination as he released one finger to take up the next. Fire lashed through her. She dropped her head back and shut her eyes tightly, but the sensations racing through her only seemed heightened.

"Tyler!" she gasped. At last he finished with her quivering pinkie.

"Yes, darling?"

Was that amusement in his voice? Or something deeper, darker? "Never mind."

Her hand fell limply from his parted lips to his chest. Slowly she turned it over, pressing her palm flat against the widest part of his body, intending to push herself off and try to recover from the safety of her own side of the bed. But she felt his heart beating beneath her hand, and the primitive rhythm held her there. *This is a man,* she thought. *He is flesh, bone, muscle and spirit.* And he was trying to communicate something vital to her, gently but insistently.

She pressed her fingertips along his breast bone, discovering the places it was the hardest, and where it left off and became muscle on either side. Coarse black hair curled between her trembling fingertips as she stroked him. She was no longer afraid. She was too busy listening for his message and learning his body. There was more of it. She glanced down to where the sheet draped across his hips.

"Touch anywhere you like," he whispered.

"Oh, I wasn't going to—"

"Yes, you were," he chuckled.

"Well, maybe," she allowed.

Tyler slowly reached for her hand and brought it down

to his waist, then laid it on the flat, hard plane of his stomach. She looked up and met his eyes. Did he really expect her to…? His gaze never left her face. Yes, he did.

"You've never even touched a man before, have you?"

She shook her head. Now he would surely think her a babe in the woods. But in her heart she now knew what she wanted. She wanted to please Tyler. Sex might become a chore for her once she learned what was required of her, but it was clear he liked it a lot. And if he took the time to show her what she must do, she'd do her darnedest to make him happy. After all, as he'd said, he was giving up other women for her.

Taking a deep breath, she slid her hand down the muscled ridges of his stomach, under the sheet. She found the elastic waist of his boxers. Trying not to think about what she would run into a few inches lower, she closed her eyes and pressed beneath the stretchy band. Her fingers met with a lush growth not unlike the curls across his chest…then a smooth, hot and very hard obstruction.

Julie froze. Now that she was here, where he wanted her…what was she supposed to do? This was where the scenes in the movie theater faded to black. She wished she'd hung around for one of those films the girls in her dorm had rented on a lark for a birthday party. They'd giggled and hooted all night long. She had left in embarrassment after her first glimpse of flesh.

"Julie?"

"Hmm?"

"Do you want to stop?"

She opened her eyes but couldn't meet his. "No."

He shifted his position slightly. "Just a suggestion then. How about wrapping those lovely fingers around me?"

She did, and she was amazed at how interestingly firm and right he felt. "What now?"

"Perhaps I should catch up," he said. She wasn't sure what he meant, until she felt his hand slide up the outside of her thigh and beneath her nightshirt. She liked the way it felt as he smoothed his palm over her hip and cupped her bottom.

"That's nice," she murmured.

"Promise to tell me when it stops being nice?"

"Yes," she agreed.

She wanted to feel all of him now that she had him. It seemed a wonderful experiment, this touching business. She learning him; he learning her. She moved her hand languidly as far down him as she could, then up again and was delighted when the motion produced a low masculine moan. She watched his face contort with pleasure, and did it again. He arched his back, and a sonorous growl of bliss rose from his throat.

She experienced a little surge of power.

Julie was so intrigued by the shapes and textures of Tyler, and her newfound ability to control him, she hardly noticed when his hand moved from her bottom to the front of her hip then slipped, as smoothly as a swallow sailing between dusk and dawn, between her thighs. His palm came to rest warmly over her feminine mound. Only when the warmth down low in her body intensified to a pulsing need did she shift her attention from Tyler's anatomy to her own.

Her eyes stayed open now, watching his, as he watched hers. She lay back on the pillow and he rose up over her, holding her in his steel-gray gaze. Gently, he touched the outer lips of her flesh. She felt something quiver inside. He pressed higher, a bare inch between delicate folds, and held his fingertips there, unmoving.

She blinked up at him, sensing he would plunge deeper if she let him, trusting he would stop if she asked. Her fingers tightened around him another notch, granting him permission.

His answering grin was both reassuring and wicked. As he began to stroke her, she felt her body responding, flowing with heat and moisture, the sensations achingly sweet. She moved her hand along him with more confidence and felt him swell again.

Julie struggled to find words to tell him that, however uncomfortable it might be for her, she wanted him inside her. She needed him there, because for as long as she could remember, she'd always felt empty and now she longed to be complete. Tyler, only Tyler had the power to make her whole. She ran her hand up then down him again and again, riding an agonizing wave as she let a pleading whimper escape her lips and the room around her swirled with prism flashes of color.

A roar not unlike that of an injured wild creature shattered her rapture. It took a moment for her to realize the sound had come from Tyler. Suddenly his warmth escaped her, her hand lay open beside her, and she sensed he was no longer tangled in the sheets with her.

With a sharp gasp, she blinked, trying to clear pink smoke from her eyes. He was standing beside the bed, pulling up his boxers. She lay sprawled in a cloud of bedclothes, her T-shirt up above her waist.

"What's wrong?" Her voice shook. Between her thighs, the tender flesh felt hot and swollen with anticipation. She tugged the shirt down self-consciously.

"I'm sorry." Tyler was breathing so hard air rasped in and out of his lungs. "Damn, I'm so sorry."

"Why? I don't understand." Tears stung the back of her eyelids.

He shook his head at her, and his eyes were darker, more determined than she'd ever seen them. "I promised we'd wait until after the wedding. But I want all of you, lady."

"Oh." His words initially thrilled her, but then she thought, if he wanted me as badly as I want him, he'd forget about schedules. He was pulling on his robe. She had to stop him. "Aren't you coming back to bed?"

He laughed but there was no humor in the sound. "If I stay in that bed with you one more second, lady—" He broke off and raked a hand through tousled hair. "I just don't think I can sleep here tonight."

"Where are you going?" Her body felt energized, needful, ready for whatever mysteries Tyler had to offer.

"Not far. I'll be out on the couch."

"Please stay." Her whispered words hovered in the air between them.

He hesitated, his eyes drifting toward the spot on the bed beside her that had been his moments before. "No. Believe me, I can't. I wouldn't be very gentle in the state I'm in." He touched an imaginary hat brim with two fingers and gave her a reassuring smile. "Later, ma'am."

That was when Julie knew she loved him.

She lay back against the pillows and smelled Tyler in them. She touched the place on the bed beside her, still warm from his body. "Julie Parker," she whispered, "for better or worse, you are definitely short one heart."

The next morning Julie woke with a start, threw on her bathrobe and hurried out to the living room to find the couch empty. Her heart sank. He'd already left for work.

"Good morning."

She spun around, grinning. No, he hadn't!

Tyler looked over his shoulder at her through the kitchen doorway. He was already dressed for work, done with breakfast and rinsing off his dishes in the sink. He gave her what passed as a smile.

"Looks like you didn't get much sleep," she commented, observing the shadows beneath his eyes as she joined him in the kitchen.

"You don't look very well-rested yourself. It's early, why don't you go back to bed for a couple of hours." He dried his hands and started toward her, then seemed to have second thoughts about the wisdom of putting her within reach.

"I'm used to rising early," she said. "I'd rather stay up. Will you be working all day?" There was nothing she'd rather do than coax him back into bed with her, if not now then later.

Their eyes met across the countertop that separated them. Tyler's expression shifted, intensified, then softened. She could almost read his thoughts. Almost. If she were to guess, she'd say he still wanted her, and that thought pleased her immensely.

"I was thinking of taking the afternoon off." He watched her expression speculatively. "We could drive out to Lightfoot's Plateau. You'd like it. The Spanish included it on an early map of the region. There's an adobe structure Shane believes was built around 1795 by our Papago ancestors at the mouth of a cave. You can see for miles across the desert from there. It's a beautiful spot."

She smiled. "I'd love that."

"Good." He crossed quickly in front of her into the living room and gathered up a long canvas satchel that looked as if it might contain rolls of blueprints, and a leather jacket. "If you're bored, call Kate. She'll be up and looking for trouble by eight o'clock. You'll be doing my mother a favor if you get her out of the house for a few hours."

"Maybe I will," Julie agreed, delighted with the idea.

Tyler turned back to look at her one last time before heading out the door. "I like your hair that way. Does something for your face."

Then he was gone, and the room seemed suddenly

empty. The world seemed empty. "God help me," she groaned collapsing onto the couch where his blanket and pillow still lay in a heap. She thrust her face into them and breathed in his scent.

She hadn't meant to fall in love with the man. It was supposed to be a business arrangement. The only way love ever worked was when both participants loved equally. Tyler might be able to tolerate or even enjoy her in bed, but the man wasn't falling in love with her.

Yes, he was momentarily intrigued by the idea of teaching her about sex. That would be a power trip for any male. But love—that was something very different. Once the excitement of being her bedroom guide wore off, he'd treat her differently.

She didn't think she could bear to see that brilliant, intoxicating light in his eyes dim. How much wiser it would be to leave now, before he stopped being sweet to her. Leave now before the flirtation turned to boredom, then disdain. If she were the one to break off their engagement, she'd never need to feel the pain of his rejection.

But she'd promised. She'd told Tyler, his parents and Kate she would go through with the wedding. She'd allowed him to buy her a ring, and she'd allowed his grandmother to make a gift of a wedding gown. And Julie had never broken a promise in her life. So she would just have to stay long enough to make her word good.

How long after that could she risk staying with Tyler in Pueblo? A month? A week? Even less? Julie sighed.

And what about her baby? Could she possibly remain in Pueblo long enough for Tyler to give her a child? If it happened fast, maybe she'd be able to cling to enough pride to walk away from him and his powerful family. Yes, if she waited just until she knew she was pregnant.... Maybe she could go home with her child and the sweet memories of the brief time she'd spent with the most fascinating man she'd ever met. At least then she'd have kept her soul.

But how would Tyler feel about her desertion? He probably wouldn't even miss her, she reasoned. He'd have what he originally wanted—a marriage on paper to satisfy his family. As far as she knew, nothing had been said about *how long* he must remain married. Devlin and Jasmine couldn't very well blame him if his bride walked out on him when he'd done nothing wrong.

For the next hour Julie puttered around the condo, straightening up, cleaning out the refrigerator, wiping down the already spotless stove top and counters simply to fill time. Her heart felt heavy, knowing that this home she was making for Tyler wouldn't be hers for long. Borrowed time, she thought. Precious minutes, that's all we'll ever have together.

At eight o'clock she telephoned the ranch, hoping Tyler had been right and she wouldn't wake anyone. The maid's voice answered brightly.

"Hello, Louisa," Julie said, "is Kate up yet? This is Julie Parker."

"Oh, yes, Miss Julie, she is right here with me in the kitchen. We are just having coffee. I get her for you."

Kate's voice almost immediately zinged through the line. "Good morning, my dear! I was hoping I'd hear from you before too many days. The arrangements are coming along beautifully. Are you excited?"

"Yes," she replied and realized she actually was. The wedding still didn't feel real to her, but she couldn't help looking forward to that one spectacular day.

"I brought the gown home with me, it's beautiful," Kate said. "And you're ready for the rehearsal and dinner this evening?"

Julie hesitated, all of her many doubts fluttering through

her mind like birds before a storm. "Yes, I suppose I'm ready."

"You don't sound very happy. Is something wrong, my dear?"

Julie winced. Was she so transparent that even a stranger could read her thoughts? "It's nothing. I'm just at loose ends this morning. Tyler is taking the afternoon off, but until then—"

"I know exactly what you need," Kate exclaimed. "I'll pick you up in twenty minutes and take you to a rather elite club, reserved for us ladies. There's discreet space to work out a bit, and a lovely sauna and whirlpool. You can't hole up in Tyler's little shoebox of a condo all day. It will drive you crazy. Here you can exercise, meet some of the other women in Pueblo, relax. It's more of a social club than a gymnasium. I think you'll like it."

Julie had never set foot in any sort of health club. She couldn't have afforded membership. And she had her doubts about feeling comfortable in one. But for Kate, she'd try.

"The spa is my second home in Pueblo, particularly when Sterling has business that keeps him away. A light workout three days a week, and I can keep up with little Lisa and soon, I hope, my other great-grandchildren. Are you two planning on having children soon?"

"Very soon, I hope," she answered truthfully. But how could she tell this lovely woman that when she did conceive, she would be taking her great-grandbaby away?

"Oh, that's wonderful," Kate said. "I'll bet your and Tyler's babies will be beautiful."

"Yes," Julie agreed. But she couldn't help realize now how much Kate, Devlin and Jasmine would hate her when she walked out of their world with Tyler's child.

Seven

"There it is," Tyler said, pointing across the desert toward a low rise of red sandstone on the horizon. Every time he came here, he felt a special thrill. "Lightfoot's Plateau."

Julie stared at this place held sacred by his ancestors. "How majestic."

"The Lightfoot family was guardian of the plateau for centuries. But when Natasha Lightfoot gave birth out of wedlock to my father and uncle, her parents refused to let her inherit the land and sold it to Brad Rowan's grandparents. My cousin Isabelle is engaged to Brad, and he's promised the property as her wedding present."

"What a romantic idea," Julie commented.

Tyler shrugged. "It's the least Rowan can do. His family has neglected it for decades, but the cave inside the plateau has continued to be a spiritual retreat for local tribes."

Julie squinted at the rising hill before them. "I don't see a cave yet."

"The adobe shelter protecting the entrance will come into view as we round the plateau."

Tyler at last eased the truck to a stop, jumped down from the cab and was around to the passenger side before Julie could open her door. He wondered at the change in her mood since the night before. Rather than becoming more relaxed when she was around him, as he had hoped, she'd begun to draw back within herself again. Yet when he'd asked if anything was wrong, she simply shrugged him off.

During difficult times, he'd often sought out the ancient cave. Maybe being here would help her, too. "When I was a boy, I used to come out here and play with my friends."

"Are you sure it's all right for me to go inside? Seeing I'm not a Papago?" Julie asked.

He smiled at her. "You're the perfect person to be here with me," he said, taking her hand in his. "Legend has it the cave guides the heart. My ancestors came here as couples to pledge themselves to each other forever."

To Tyler's knowledge, only one member of his family in recent times had strayed from those sacred vows. His grandparents had separated during the troubled years following the tragic death of their child. At least emotion wouldn't enter his own marriage. He and Julie each had a vested interest in this union. No hearts involved. Which was fortunate, because he could imagine himself caring deeply about a woman like Julie. If he let himself...and he wouldn't.

Yet, as he took Julie's hand and they climbed together over the rough terrain, following the steps of his ancestors, he couldn't help feeling an inexplicable, almost mystical attraction to the woman at his side. To hold her at his side and keep her there, safe—that was what he wanted. Julie had never in her life had a protector, and he wanted to be hers. If she'd open herself to him and learn to trust him, he'd do his level best to be there for her. *Not because I love her,* he silently told the spirits watching over them, *but because I want to be a friend.*

He lit the kerosene lantern he knew he'd find just inside the opening of the adobe structure sheltering the cave's mouth. "Legends say when a man and woman stand together in the cave, bound by love, and swear fidelity—they will never part." He held the lantern high and watched Julie walk around the walls of the cave, touching her fingertips to the ancient petroglyphs drawn in plant and animal stains or scraped into the surface with rough implements.

"This is a wonderful place," she whispered. Her eyes were wide and glistening in the soft orange glow of the lamp. "You can feel the presence of generations here. It's almost like being in an old church...so beautiful and private and peaceful."

"Yes." He could feel it, too.

But he also felt other things. It was as if he was being drawn deeper into a destiny he hadn't foreseen. The sensation of oneness with Julie intensified. Was marriage more than a legal status and complication to his life?

Something inside Tyler fought the idea of fate seizing control of his life. Impulsively, he strode across the cavern, took Julie's hands in his own and knelt on the cold, hard ground, pulling her down to her knees facing him.

"I swear by the spirits of my ancestors," he intoned with mock solemnity, "to hold you, Julie Parker, as my one true wife. To always cherish—"

"No!" she screamed, glaring in horror at him. "Don't do that!" Tears filled her pretty hazel eyes before spilling down her cheeks. Before he could reassure her that he was just joking, she yanked her hands out of his and leapt to her feet.

"What? I was just fooling around. You know, because of the magic this place is supposed to have." He stood up, reached for her hand again, but she snapped it away from him. "They're just old legends—like some cultures' fairy tales."

"No," she insisted with surprising emotion. "You shouldn't make light of your heritage." Tears streamed down her face now, and she didn't bother to wipe them off.

"I didn't mean any harm," he protested.

She shook her head violently at him and turned away.

Tyler went to her, wrapped his arms around her then turned her against his chest while she wept softly. "Tell me why this place and what I've said are so important to you."

"I can't explain," she choked out.

"Try."

Julie looked up at him tearfully. "You have such a wonderful family with rich traditions. I would give all I own to have had what you grew up with."

He looked down at her, astonished. She was serious.

"I'm sorry," he said softly. "Sometimes I forget how lucky I am." He splayed the wide fingers of one hand across the back of her head and smoothed down the mussed strands of her silky hair. Then he did it again, just because it felt good. "Forgive me, Julie."

She gazed up at him, a lost child, and he wondered if there was something more she still hadn't told him and was keeping in her own heart.

"Remember, my family will soon be yours, too," he whispered.

She nodded but said nothing. He consoled himself with the thought that, in time, he'd learn her moods and how to soothe her when she was troubled. They had time... plenty of time.

If Julie had fears, he would seek them out and conquer them. It didn't seem particularly important to him that neither of them could say the words other couples said: *I love you.* He wasn't even sure such a thing as love really existed. But maybe Julie was right about legends and vows. There seemed to be something powerful at work in this sacred place, something drawing him to her. He certainly hadn't meant to be irreverent. He'd just needed a way to break the tension.

Tyler lifted Julie's chin and looked down into her eyes—mossy-green with flecks of amber in the lantern's flickering light. "I'm going to enjoy coming home to you," he murmured.

She flung her arms around his neck and pulled him down with such unexpected strength, he didn't have a chance to take a breath before her mouth locked over his. "I don't...don't want...don't want to leave!" she cried in little gasps between urgent kisses.

"Leave?" He chuckled, pressing his lips to the faint worry lines across her forehead. "We don't have to go anywhere. We can stay here for a while if you like it."

She looked up at him as if she was going to say something more, but didn't. "Yes," she agreed at last, "for a while. Here." Unexpectedly, she stepped back a few paces and pulled her bulky sweater up over her head and off. Spreading it on the stone floor, she sat down then reached for his hand and drew him down beside her onto a corner of the soft wool.

He was amused and pleased by her gentle insistence on remaining in the cave.

"Would it be offensive to your ancestors if we...you know...?" she asked timidly.

He raised a puzzled brow. She couldn't mean...? "Made love in the cave?"

Julie nodded quickly.

Tyler roared with laughter. "I expect when my grandfather used to speak of couples pledging themselves to one another here, he was referring to a physical as well as a spiritual union. We Papago are a very passionate people."

"Will you?"

"Make love to you here?" Another unexpected mood swing? But this one was a delightful surprise. Then it struck him that he'd brought no protection with him. "Are you sure you're ready?" he asked doubtfully.

"Yes." Her lips settled into a firm line, and her eyes held steadily on his. "I don't want to wait for the wedding."

"You won't be very comfortable on this hard floor. I don't want to hurt you."

"You won't, Tyler." She gave him a charmingly lopsided smile. An attempt at being brave, he suspected. "I thought I saw a blanket in the back of your truck."

"I don't know how long the kerosene will last," he said. "Maybe an hour or two."

"Wouldn't that be long enough?" she asked innocently.

He wanted to throw himself on top of her that very instant. She looked utterly delicious with the light of the lantern tossing golden shadows across her features. But he knew they'd end up bruised and scraped from the cave floor if he didn't go for a blanket.

She had just better not change her mind before he got back!

Tyler raced down the side of the hill to the truck and hastily fetched two hand-loomed blankets from the bed of the truck. When he returned, out of breath and beaded with sweat, Julie had removed her shoes and was kneeling before a wall, tracing the rough, faded lines of a cave design with her fingertips. She seemed utterly calm, until she turned to look at him. Then a passion as fierce as the desert sun fixed on him. Tyler hesitated for a moment in the cave's mouth before shaking out the blankets and laying them one atop the other. "No one will disturb us," he whispered.

"I know," she said, sitting in the middle of the woven pattern. "It feels safe here."

"Safer than the condo?"

She puckered her lips and gave him a strange look. "Yes, in a way. More than that, it feels like the right place to make our baby."

A lump the size of Texas swelled in Tyler's chest as he gazed down on her. Emotions bombarded him. Perhaps it wasn't really lust he'd just now observed in her eyes. Maybe all that mattered to her, still, was the baby she'd wanted for so long. A family. And he was the vehicle to get what she wanted. He was just a tool.

Tyler felt the sting of rejection as fiercely as if she'd struck him.

He nearly turned and walked out of the cave, but stopped himself. Now wasn't the time to surrender to male pride. If Julie didn't love him, what was so bloody wrong with that? He hadn't wanted that in the beginning, and he shouldn't feel the loss now. Tonight he would make love to his Julie the best he knew how. Tomorrow they would marry and they'd both have what they wanted. At least he would. The baby, her share of the bargain, might take some time.

Tyler lowered himself beside her. "You realize," he murmured, "a woman doesn't usually get pregnant on the

first shot. We might have to work at this for a while."
With any luck, he thought, it will take months...years.

She smiled, suddenly shy again. "I know, but don't you
think that if it's meant to happen, it will be here?"

She was beautifully naive. So much so he hated to
change her. But fulfilling her destiny as a woman was going to change her. No doubt about that.

She stretched out on the blankets and gazed trustingly
up at him. "Should I do anything?"

"Yes," he said, smiling, "kiss your husband-to-be as if
you love him more than life itself."

Her eyes widened in the split second before he lowered
his head and pressed his lips over her cool mouth. Her
shock didn't last long. He felt her lengthen her neck, tip
her head back and open her mouth to his. He tasted her,
delicately at first. Unable to satisfy himself he plunged
deeper, with a thirst that surprised him.

Julie looped her arms around his neck and pulled him
down on top of her. Suddenly, he couldn't recall what she
was wearing, what he was wearing...or where they were.
Everything other than her body and his evaporated in a
blue mist of passion. He let his hands explore, sliding beneath layers of clothing, seeking out the warmth of her
flesh wherever they traveled. He found her breasts, rubbed
the callused pads of his thumbs across already peaked nip-
ples, enjoyed feeling her arch into him.

Each kiss seemed to last an eternity, yet none was long
enough to satisfy him. He felt suddenly overwhelmed by
her, as if she were the aggressor, the seductress—although
she had done nothing but react to his touch. He'd never
felt like this before; it shocked him. And confused him,
because he liked this feeling of not being in control. Everything felt fresh, new, intensely erotic—forbidden yet
perfectly natural.

Yes, there had been other women. Too many, perhaps. But something about Julie was uniquely stirring. A primal connection seemed to grow between them, filling the cave. She matched his rhythms and hunger, met the flow of his hormones with her own, driving him higher. Silently begging him to be gentle while inviting him to be wicked—the contrast was delicious.

Tyler lifted her blouse and slipped her bra above her breasts. A tiny flinching motion from her reminded him of how new and mysterious this was to her in a way he, as a man, would never understand. "I won't hurt you," he breathed as he lowered his head and smoothed his lips from her navel upward across butter-soft flesh. Her stomach muscles quivered; he quieted them with the gentle pressure of his cheek then continued distributing kisses.

"I want to kiss you everywhere. *Everywhere,*" he repeated with emphasis.

"Oh." It was a combination moan and yip of surprise.

"Is that a yes or a no?"

"Ah…oh my…" She groaned deep in her throat as his mouth closed over her nipple and drew the dark, round circle of flesh between the sharp edges of his teeth. "Yes-s-s-s," she hissed as her body tightened along every feminine muscle from fingertips to toes.

He was delighted and toyed mercilessly with her breasts with the tip of his tongue and his lips and teeth, until her breathing grew ragged and raspy. Until Julie let out a sharp cry she choked off by thrusting the knuckles of one hand against her open mouth. He wasn't sure that she recognized the significance of what had just happened—this first of many climaxes he'd give her. But he was delighted she was so responsive to him. He felt a surge of power, followed quickly by a warning voice. *Slowly. Slowly now.*

Too much too soon, and he'd frighten her. He didn't

want to have to abort like the other night. Above all, he didn't want her to feel cheap or dirty or used. Tyler needed her to know how richly she was cherished at this moment, but he wasn't sure he knew how to show her.

Slowly, he stripped off her clothing, piece by piece, until he could see every inch of her pale skin in the orange glow of the lantern. It was the first time nothing had separated him from her. He ran his hand down the side of her body, past her waist, slowing to savor the delicious curve of her hip. His palm smoothed across the top of her thigh to cup her. There, he forced himself to wait and meet her glazed eyes...and hold them. Just long enough to let her know she still had the power to end this with the tiniest shake of her head.

She smiled then let her eyes drift closed.

He angled his hand to stretch his fingers cautiously toward the delicate center of her womanhood. He found what he had expected. Julie was already drenched with her honeyed response to him.

"Now what am I going to do with you?" he whispered, grinning down at her. "You've beat me once already."

Her eyes flew open in astonishment. "You mean I...already? I did, really?"

"Really."

She looked worried and clutched anxiously at his shoulders. "But you didn't even... I mean, does that mean it's all over?"

He shook his head slowly. "Not by a long shot, darlin'."

Her lips lifted in the sweetest smile he'd ever known. "Good. Now kiss me, husband-to-be, as if you loved me more than life itself."

And he did.

He kissed her with such feeling that he more than half

believed it was true. And as he kissed her deeper and deeper still, he moved his fingers up between the delicate folds of silky skin flowing with her ecstasy, and he carefully pressed against the seal of her womanhood until he felt it give way. She let out only the smallest whimper of pain. When he tried to lift his head to catch a glimpse of her face to make sure she was all right, she pulled him down and captured his mouth and kissed him long and hard.

"Are you ready?" he asked at last. He knew that he'd prepared her physically, but emotionally he could only hope for the best. If he did anything too fast, too hard, too anything—he'd frighten her, and he'd never get her back and never forgive himself.

In answer, she reached down and unzipped his jeans, then shyly touched the front of his briefs. The ridge of his manhood stood clearly evident beneath the fabric. She looked up at him as if for permission.

He winked at her.

Blushing, she pressed her hand over him. Even through the fabric he could feel her trembling, and a lick of fire shot through him.

Don't take too long! a voice inside his head begged.

But as urgently as he ached to lose himself inside her, he also wanted this time to last forever. These few moments before she finally understood what it was all about. These final precious seconds before her innocence was gone forever and she figured out that he was neither more nor less than any other man. For now, she was looking at him as if he were a god, and tomorrow he would be just Tyler Fortune, a guy who could read a blueprint and weld an I-beam. He desperately wanted to hold on to that worship in her eyes.

Tyler edged his jeans and briefs down over his hips, revealing himself to her, full and heavy with need.

"Tyler," she breathed and reached out for him, less shyly than before. When her fingers closed around him this time, they felt warm and were no longer shaking. She moved her hand along him, and Tyler dropped his head back and closed his eyes on the agonizing bliss.

He quickly clamped his hand over hers.

"I did something wrong?" she asked, sounding worried.

"No," he ground out. "That was…perfect. But do it one more time and we won't be making any babies today."

She smiled a little too coyly for his comfort. "Oh?" Already she was learning.

"Yes, oh." He kissed her quickly on the lips, easing her back down onto the blanket. When he was over her, he looked into her eyes and said, "Now you can let go."

She did, but her hand—intentionally, he was sure—brushed downward across sensitive flesh, flicking her fingernails lightly over intimate regions, sending him miles into the stratosphere. The woman's a natural, he thought as he soared. How could he have ever assumed that making love to Julie was going to be a chore? This was a responsibility he'd enjoy for a long time.

But now he must concentrate on making her first experience as special as he could. She'd already climaxed once, at least. He wanted to define her limits, discover how many times was just right for her. Once was generally all he needed. With her, he'd be sorely tempted to try for more. But he'd better make sure he thoroughly satisfied her first before taking his own pleasure.

Her hands came down to rest lightly on his hips as he guided himself between her thighs. He felt her tighten for a moment, then relax as her eyes sought out his and found reassurance. "It won't hurt anymore," he whispered. "We've already taken care of that."

She nodded her understanding, opened herself to him, and he moved inside her in one long, slow passage. He quickly reached her limit.

"I'm too small," she whispered apologetically.

"You're just right."

"But you—"

"—and I fit one another," he finished for her. "And the more times I make you mine, the farther I will be able to go until you take all of me. It will happen. Believe me."

Tyler smoothed tendrils of glossy hair away from her face, tenderly kissed her hot cheeks, sweet mouth, silky throat. He moved within her in the timeless rhythm that links man and woman, joining them in a single moment of euphoria and legacy of love that foretells new generations.

He felt her instinctively lift her long, elegant legs and wrap them around his hips, opening herself a little more, pulling him deeper. He held on for as long as he could, reveling in her fire and her sweet whimpers, burying his face in the soft cove between her throat and shoulder as he lost count of the times she rose in ecstasy then settled limply beneath him, only to rise again.

Flames engulfed him and burned, burned, burned…until all he could see was a red wash before his eyes, mounting like a tidal wave. And all he could feel was building pressure in his loins and a blaze so intense he'd be consumed in another moment.

He felt Julie quiver violently then close tightly around him as she climaxed once more. Attempting to hold off any longer would be futile. He arched and lengthened his strong back, supporting himself above her on the heels of his hands, gripping the blankets in rock-hard fists. As he thrust fiercely into her one final time, he released his very soul in a long hot stream. From his open mouth, the echoes of a warrior's cry filled the cavern as Tyler Lightfoot Fortune claimed his woman under the approving gaze of his ancestors.

It seemed to Julie that someone, at some time during her life, definitely should have prepared her for this.

Or maybe there was no way of understanding the sensations, hues, heights and valleys and indescribable feelings that assaulted a woman when she freed herself to be with a man. All reservations had flown from her heart the moment Tyler began making love to her that afternoon. She'd never looked back, never questioned if what she was doing was right or intelligent or risky.

She hadn't intentionally set aside her fears. Trusting him was something she couldn't help doing. It was the first time she'd ever let herself experience a situation without analyzing, making excuses, or feeling awkward about how she walked, talked or breathed. In Tyler's arms, joined with him, she had simply existed on the most sublime level imaginable.

Existing seemed enough. Existing seemed plenty.

Now she lay very still beneath him, feeling his heart beat nearly as rapidly as hers, but with a deeper resonance. Feeling him take in and release each breath, loudly, with more than a little effort. He felt heavy over her, but she liked the pressure. He still felt hard and full within her, and she liked that, too. She tried to imagine standing up and walking out of the cave alone, without Tyler touching her, staying with her, remaining a part of her...and she couldn't.

Does he feel this, too? she wondered. This magic? Sadly, she supposed not. Men, by reputation, were supposed to function sexually without all the emotional baggage women attached to physical relations.

She lifted a hand and rested it gently at the back of his neck, touching the short hairs at the nape, soaking up the last sensations of his body in, over, around her. He'd done his duty, even before the wedding. If she became pregnant as a result of this night, he need never touch her again. As flattering as he'd been, she had no doubt that most of his comments were intended to relax and reassure her. Men like Tyler Fortune who dated models, heiresses, the daughters of powerful politicians—they didn't fall all over themselves for an assistant branch librarian.

Nevertheless, he had seemed to enjoy himself, and, if she correctly read his present inert posture, he was fully satisfied. A small, proud part of her congratulated herself. It might never happen again, but she sure as heck hadn't disappointed the man this time. Julie grinned.

"What's so funny?" Tyler mumbled thickly against her throat.

"How did you know I was smiling?"

"I could feel the muscles in your face move."

"Maybe I was making a face because you're crushing me," she countered.

"Am I?" He started to lift away from her.

"No. I'm just teasing."

"I was afraid of that."

"What?" she asked, concerned by his tone.

"Already I've changed you. Before we made love, you weren't capable of teasing…no sense of humor whatsoever."

"I beg your pardon!" She gasped and pushed him away, but as he fell backward, rolling to one side, he was laughing.

"See? Another change. Your inherent violent nature is showing itself now."

She shook her head at him, laughing joyfully. "I may be a lot of things, but violent isn't one of them."

He seemed to drift away from her then, for just a moment as he pulled up his jeans and tucked in his shirt, which he'd never taken off. She dressed, then sat down again, waiting for him to say something. But he was standing in the middle of the cave looking around at the walls as if searching for a personal message among the rusty red, black, and ochre petroglyphs.

"Is something wrong?" she asked.

"No." He shrugged. "It's just that I should have explained something about my history before we did this."

A tiny ache in her heart shattered the moment. The passion and delightfully intimate humor suddenly seemed miles away. Now was the moment he'd break her heart. "You've been with other women," she murmured. "It's all right."

"It's not all right," he said tightly. "I don't want you to worry about certain things."

What was he trying to say? "I don't understand."

"Like I've said, I've cultivated the playboy image. It was convenient. Until recently, that image kept marriage at bay." He paused. "I just want to reassure you that it's been over six months since my last...encounter." He smiled diplomatically at her. "And when I decided to register with Soulmate, I asked my doctor to run the appropriate tests because I wanted to be able to assure my future wife that I was perfectly healthy, even though I'd always practiced safe sex and knew what the results would be."

She nodded, grateful that he was being so forthright and considerate. "I wouldn't have even thought of being tested."

"No need in your case." He smiled as if this pleased him.

Julie sat on the cave floor, tucking her toes into her shoes and observing him. She wanted to ask him if she had lived up to his expectations in other ways, but didn't know how. "You would tell me, wouldn't you, Tyler? I mean if I wasn't any good at...you know..."

He laughed with gusto that warmed her insides. "My darling woman, you don't have a clue how marvelous you are, do you?" He hauled her to her feet and enclosed her in a crushing bear hug. And when she was about to turn blue from lack of oxygen, he moved her away from him to study her face as if absorbing and placing in memory every eyelash, each tiny line and soft contour. "We'd better get back now. Don't want to be late for your own bridal dinner."

Eight

Julie woke on the morning of her wedding to the sound of a telephone ringing. Tyler moved on the bed beside her to answer it.

"No, don't come here. I agree we have to talk, but—" His voice sounded tense and sharp as he raked splayed fingers through sleep-mussed hair.

Julie rolled out of bed and pulled on her robe. Wanting to give him some privacy during what sounded like an important conversation, she went into the kitchen to make coffee. She sliced wedges of a maple-walnut coffeecake she'd baked the day before, then set two places at the cozy kitchen table.

"Well, sure, it's important." She could hear Tyler's raised voice from the bedroom. "That's why I was about to suggest you meet me at the site. I can be there in twenty minutes."

Julie sighed as she sat down and took a sip of coffee. He was planning to work on their wedding day?

The phone slammed down loudly. A moment later, Tyler appeared in the kitchen doorway in his boxers. Despite his obviously less than romantic mood, she felt a curl of warmth within her at the sight of his broad chest and flat, muscled stomach. Memories of the night before returned. They'd made love again after the rehearsal dinner.

"Something's wrong," she said, not bothering to put it as a question.

Tyler nodded, rubbing the bridge of his nose with one knuckle. "That was Link Templeton. It seems he has come up with additional evidence that Mike Dodd's death wasn't an accident."

"Then there's no doubt someone intentionally killed the man?" she asked, putting down her cup.

"Yes, but so far there seems to be no logical motive. Mike was a hardworking guy. Everyone liked him."

"Well, you must go then," she said regretfully, looking down at the intimate pair of coffee cups on the table. It was so nice to put food on a table for two, instead of just one.

"I had hoped we'd spend the morning together," he said as if reading her thoughts. The glimmer in his dark eyes thrilled her. "Alone. Here."

She felt herself blush. The mere thought of making love with Tyler yet again drove up her blood pressure. "Maybe," she suggested shyly, "there will be time later."

"Kate has this shindig scheduled for one o'clock," he reminded her.

Julie stood up and walked around the table to lace her fingers around Tyler's neck. "Maybe you'll be able to come back in an hour or so?" She felt positively wicked, and she loved this new addition to her previously limited stock of emotions.

"I hope so." Looping his strong arms around her waist, he pulled her to him. "Will you be here?"

Julie smiled. "You can bet on it."

He kissed her then returned to the bedroom to dress. On his way out the door fifteen minutes later, he kissed her again but she could see that his mind was already in another place. She stood at the bay window and watched the man she would soon marry drive away, and a sense of deep, irreparable loss enveloped her. Before she knew she loved Tyler Fortune, she had been able to look on their relationship so simply.

But he'd made love to her. They hadn't just had sex. Hadn't just performed the required physical act to produce a baby. They'd made love—at least *she* had. And no amount of reasoning could banish the feelings she cherished for him now. He had filled a void in her life. He made it easier to smile, to hope, to dream and even, it sometimes seemed, to breathe. Tyler Fortune possessed her. She was no longer her own person. And that terrified her.

If he ever walked out of her life because he fell in love, *really in love* with another woman…she would still love him. If he grew tired of her and stopped touching her in his magical ways, she would still want him. If he lost himself in his work for months on end, forgetting she existed, it would make no difference to the way she felt. He was a part of her, inside her body and her mind, wrapped around her soul.

Another thought, just as threatening, occurred to her: What if something terrible happened to Tyler? Something that took him from her even if he wanted to stay? If it was true that someone did murder his foreman, then what was to stop that person from killing again? Tyler had said it himself—no one knew why the person had done it. And he'd also told her there had been opposition to the hospital. If someone was insane enough to kill one person, hoping to stop construction, was there any reason why the killer would stop at one victim? And who might be a better target than Tyler, the muscle behind the project?

An icy hand gripped her—squeezing until all the lovely memories of his body, his laugh, his touch were gone. If anything happened to him, the brief glimpse of happiness she'd known would never be repeated.

Julie stared out the window, steadying herself against the wooden frame. So very easily…it could all be gone. Yet, why should that bother her, when she'd already made up her mind to leave before Tyler or fate could deal her a blow from which she'd never recover?

The string quartet played a sensuous adagio by Bach as Julie stepped out into the garden. Adele spread Julie's train behind her in a fan to follow her up the band of white silk stretching along the ground from the patio doorway to the makeshift altar in front of a stone fountain. Lisa led the procession, scattering rose petals before her.

As guests turned in their seats to catch a glimpse of the bride, Julie drew a sharp breath at their number. They were all strangers except for the members of Tyler's family she'd already met and a few friends from Houston. Her East Coast cousins hadn't been able to make the trip. Julie silently thanked Kate for doing away with the traditional seating arrangement—one side of the aisle for the bride's family and friends, the other for the groom's. Instead, guests were clustered throughout the garden, like colorful flowers opening to the sun on a warm spring day.

Julie's heart beat faster as she looked up the aisle toward

the minister, half expecting Tyler not to be there. She wouldn't have blamed him if he'd gotten cold feet and not shown. After all, who was she to deserve this royal treatment?

But Tyler was there. He was there and he was perfect. Her heart stopped for a ten-count when their eyes met. She felt as if every joint in her body turned liquid in that moment. He was beautiful. He was smiling at her. And, at least for this day, he was hers.

Tyler wore an elegant black tuxedo that she was sure must have been tailored for him. The jacket's shoulders molded his own. Lapels followed the swell of his chest and tapered to nothing at his tight, hard waist. The trouser legs were slim cut, and she knew little space came between him and the fabric, for she remembered vividly the powerful muscles of his thighs. His smile widened when he saw her, and she melted.

Devlin Fortune took her arm just in time to steady her. "Ready?" her new father-in-law whispered in her ear. His eyes were laughing at her as if he knew how nervous she was.

What in heaven's name was she doing here? How had she ever dared to think she could go through with this ruse? Maybe if it had been a matter of just her and Tyler eloping then living in a town where no one knew them. But she wasn't only marrying him. She was marrying this magnificent family with its history, traditions and expectations that she'd fit in.

She couldn't do it! She just couldn't—

"You're far better than he deserves…and everything he deserves," Devlin said into the whirl of her emotions as the violins segued into a stately march. "You're the best that's happened to that boy."

She stared at Devlin in astonishment, but the idea of

arguing with him didn't even occur to her. His words held a ring of authority. If he believed in them as a couple, maybe they actually had a chance. Maybe.

"Thank you," she whispered. Dropping her eyes to the river of silk at her toes, Julie murmured a silent prayer then moved a step forward on Devlin Fortune's arm. Closer and closer to Tyler, as the regal strains of two violins, a viola and cello lifted her hopes and her chin.

There was something she couldn't define in Tyler's gaze as he watched her approach him. She wondered if he was remembering the cave, thinking about the firelight shadowing off their bodies as they lay together in the timeless melding of two bodies into a single spirit. No matter what happened to them in the months to come—she would never forget the look in his eyes the moment he'd made her his. Nothing, she vowed, would rob her of that beautiful memory.

Nothing.

Julie became aware that they'd stopped moving. They had reached the makeshift altar. Before leaving her side, Devlin squeezed her hand once. Tyler reached out, enfolded her cold fingers in his and drew her to his side.

Suddenly everything seemed to happen so fast she was unable to absorb details. The music stopped; the minister was speaking. People stood, then sat. More music, more talking. All the while, Tyler's reassuring gaze held and comforted her. She heard the minister's voice but couldn't make sense of individual words. It was as if she was listening to someone speak a beautiful foreign language; only sounds and tones conveyed his meaning. When he at last paused and looked at her expectantly, she blinked up at Tyler. He smiled and nodded at her.

"Oh, I do!" she murmured.

"And do you, Tyler Benjamin Fortune, take Julie Ann Parker to be your—"

"I do," Tyler said quickly.

The minister smiled at his eagerness, and when they'd exchanged rings and been pronounced man and wife, Tyler took Julie in his arms and kissed her long and thoroughly on the mouth until she was dizzy and gasping for breath. A cheer went up, notably from the Fortune cousins, and the guests all stood and clapped as Julie and Tyler retreated through the garden onto the shady patio at the back of the house.

"Well, Mrs. Fortune, I warned you my grandmother would make a grand affair of this," Tyler said with mock grimness. His eyes sparkled, not so much gray as a smoky blue. She could have sworn he was enjoying himself.

"I never dreamed there would be so many people!" she gasped.

"Did you notice the governor and his wife sitting beside the rose arbor?"

Julie thumped him on the chest with her fist and laughed. "Stop that."

"It's true! They were sitting beside Senator Davies and his wife. I won't list the other dignitaries if it bothers you."

She was having difficulty breathing. Her heart was racing—but not from fear. She was excited, delirious with joy! Everything seemed too good to be true, but it was real.

The ceremony had been a perfect and thrilling moment in her otherwise ordinary life. The flowers, fountains, guests and beautiful music...it was a fantasy come true. Even more amazingly, she'd lived through the experience without tripping, running into anything, stammering through her vows, or saying anything so foolish the guests would roll their eyes and say of Tyler, "Poor boy. How will he ever live with a woman like that!"

Julie swelled with pride. She was just about to tell Tyler how happy she was when Kate rushed through the patio doors, quickly followed by Devlin and Jasmine. "Oh, you two looked so gorgeous up there, I could have cried!" Kate exclaimed.

"You did cry," Devlin teased her.

"Oh, stop it, I did not. Why would I blubber on such a happy occasion as this?" She turned back to Julie and Tyler, her face glowing like a teenage girl's at her first dance. "Now, the two of you, into the parlor for photographs. Your guests will be waiting for you in the living room. If I'd known the weather would be this nice, I would have planned on having everyone stay outside. But—" she looked at her grandson knowingly "—I don't suppose it matters to you one way or another, as long as you can escape with your bride as soon as possible."

Tyler grinned, threw an arm around his grandmother's narrow shoulders and gave her a bone-crushing hug. "You know me too well, Kate darling."

Julie felt herself blushing and tried to avoid Tyler's roguish gaze.

The musicians moved inside and began a selection of Chopin, while the formal bridal portraits were taken. By the time Julie and Tyler joined their guests again, the caterer's servers were circling the room with trays of hot and cold, hearty and light delicacies. Julie selected one of everything, and it was all delicious—crab puffs, lobster crisps, spectacular little cheese whirls and luscious black caviar on tiny circles of toast.

Tyler was at her side every moment as they greeted guests. Suddenly, the musicians struck up a waltz and the floor cleared. Everyone looked around for Tyler and his new bride.

"Oh, no," Julie whispered under her breath, "I don't know how to—"

"No time like the present to learn," Tyler said with a devilish grin.

"Oh—but no, I—"

It was no use, he hauled her into his arms, placed his right hand along the curve of her spine and lifted her right hand in his left. "If you can count to three, you can waltz."

"Yeah, right," she muttered.

"Trust me. Just follow my lead."

Julie had never danced, she soon realized, with a man who actually knew how to dance. At some time in his life, Tyler Fortune had mastered the waltz with the same thorough attention to detail he gave to erecting a building. He supported her securely, her feet barely touching the floor, and when he took a long step forward, she automatically took a corresponding step backward. He moved with athletic grace. For him, dancing wasn't a matter of prissy manners. It was great sport, and he tackled it with just that attitude—chin forward, eyes directed toward the far end of the room as if the goal line waited for him there, his partner tucked firmly in his arms. He moved with aggressive ease across the room then circled back, and Julie hardly needed to think about what her feet were doing to match his long, sweeping strides.

By the time the music stopped and the faces of guests ceased swirling around her, she was breathing hard but laughing delightedly as the company clapped and whistled their approval of the newlyweds' waltz. Then it was time for everyone to join in, and the floor grew crowded.

Tyler drew her aside and picked up two crystal champagne flutes. He offered one to her, touching his lightly to her rim. "Here's to the bride, light on her feet and a good sport to boot."

"I didn't know you were such a wonderful dancer! That was amazing."

"I took just enough lessons to learn a few basic steps, as a means of surviving Kate's twice-yearly formal parties," he explained.

"But you're so good!" she exclaimed. "You even made me look good."

"That's the gentleman's job," he said gallantly, taking a long swallow of the golden bubbles. "In some cases, however, the lady herself makes the job very easy." He put an arm around her waist and pulled her close to him. "Have I told you that you make an astonishingly beautiful bride?"

She looked down into her champagne. "I'm not beautiful, it's the dress."

"Foolish woman," he murmured.

She looked up at him, afraid that he might be angry with her, but his expression was soft and thoughtful as he drained his glass and set it on a nearby tray.

"You really don't know, do you?" he asked, grazing the underside of her chin with the crook of one finger. "There aren't many women who look even vaguely attractive without makeup. You are one who does. Add a touch of lipstick and that knock-'em-dead hairstyle of yours, and you're stunning."

She suspected he was just being nice, trying to make her feel special on her wedding day. She'd always remember how kind he'd been to her, how considerate. His acceptance of her as she was, without the polish or sophistication of those women he was accustomed to...that was a gift she'd treasure always.

The party continued. At last, when Julie felt she couldn't eat another bite or dance another step, Tyler leaned over and whispered in her ear, "Time to go, Mrs. Fortune."

Mrs. Fortune. Mrs. Julie Ann Parker Fortune. How elegant that sounded!

Tyler took her hand and led her toward the corner of the room where his parents stood. Jasmine kissed her on the cheek and whispered, "You've made us so happy." Devlin shook his son's hand and looked so proud he might burst.

Rice was thrown. Shouts of best wishes followed them out the door. But Tyler stopped suddenly at the top of the steps and stared down at the circular drive. "Dear lord."

Julie followed his shocked gaze. There in front of the house was Tyler's pickup, bedecked in long strips of blue paper. Shredded blueprints, Julie thought, giggling. And replicas of tools clipped from tin sheeting dangled from the rear bumper.

"Looks as if your brother has been busy," she commented dryly.

He laughed out loud and long, until she thought he couldn't possibly still be breathing. "With help from Shane and Riley, no doubt," he managed at last. "Come on, let's get out of here before they have a chance to pull any other stunts."

Julie stuffed herself and her gown into the passenger seat, with help from Tyler. He leapt into the driver's seat and took off down the long tree-lined drive, spraying dust and gravel behind them. But as soon as they were out of sight of the house, he pulled the truck to a stop.

"What are you doing?" Julie asked.

He flung open his door and got out. "Putting my vehicle back in order." Tyler pulled off strips of paper and clanking pieces of metal. He opened the lock box in the truck bed, pulled out a rag, and wiped the soapy Just Married off the rear window.

Something inside Julie cringed and whimpered. Maybe that's what he thought he was doing, but Julie sensed his behavior meant more. The show was over. He had the wife who would guarantee his share of the Fortune estate. There was no reason to pretend for guests any longer.

"It was a lovely party," Julie murmured as he climbed back into the cab.

He glanced at her sideways and grunted something she couldn't quite make out. Her heart felt smaller, colder, wiser.

They drove toward town for several miles before Tyler spoke again. "Look, I left a lot of loose ends over at the site. I guess since we planned not to bother with a honeymoon, it doesn't matter what we do with the rest of the day."

The final remnants of her dream melted away. "I—I guess not," Julie whispered, then remembered what Kate had said about standing up to her headstrong grandson. If she didn't let him know how she felt and what she needed from him, she'd be miserable. She tried to think of words that would make Tyler understand how disappointed she was that they wouldn't be together on their wedding night.

"Listen," he said hesitantly, "I hadn't planned to leave you this soon. Don't get upset. It's just that so much has to be done in so little time." Tyler pulled the truck to a stop in front of the condo but didn't get out. "I won't stay more than a few hours."

"I understand," she said woodenly, gathering up her full satin skirt like an armload of laundry. Damn him, he wasn't even going inside with her. She'd have to cross the threshold by herself on her wedding day!

Tyler seized her arm before she could push herself out

the door. "You don't understand how important this is, Julie."

"Oh, yes, I do."

"No!" he said fiercely, dragging her back across the seat and into his arms so suddenly she lost her grip on her dress and the fabric tumbled around her into a white pool of satin. He kissed her possessively on the mouth. "I promise. I'll prove to you tonight where I really want to be."

Her heart jumped into her throat. Her mouth felt suddenly parched with anticipation, hot from his kiss. She looked up at him and was shocked to see smoldering desire in his eyes. An emotion that had nothing to do with accidents, construction or investigators.

"Really?" she breathed.

"Really. And don't bother preparing anything for dinner. I'll bring something we can share…in bed."

The news wasn't good. Link Templeton paced Tyler's office at Fortune headquarters, shaking his head of sandybrown hair as he glowered at the parquet floor passing beneath his feet. "I'm sorry as hell to spoil your wedding day like this—but I thought you and Jason should know what I've found, right away." He drew a deep breath. "Without going into details, I've discovered evidence of tampering with the braking mechanism of the elevator. And because of the close timing between when your crew left for the day, the watchman's rounds, and the hour when Dodd must have returned to the site…I'd say it had to have been an inside job."

Tyler stared incredulously at Jason, then at the private investigator the family had hired in hopes of quickly proving the foreman's death was no more than an unfortunate accident. "What are you saying? That one of my crew killed Mike?" Tyler ground out.

"It means we're not talking about some hopped-up pranksters who just happened along one night and decided to see if they could make an elevator fail," Link said. "This was planned. My guess is, they knew Dodd and knew their way around the site. It wasn't a first-time visit."

"But you can't be sure of this," Jason stated.

Link shrugged. "If you're asking me for absolute proof, I can't give it to you yet. And I can't eliminate anyone from suspicion at this point. Not even your family."

"*My* family?" Tyler couldn't believe what he was hearing. "Forget it," he snapped. "That's impossible."

"Is it?"

"No Fortune had reason to kill Dodd," Jason said.

"He was our employee," Tyler pointed out. "And a damn good one. He kept the project moving on schedule. Besides that, he got along well with nearly everyone."

"Someone didn't much like him." Link grimaced. "And until we figure out why that elevator was tampered with, and what brought Dodd down to the site in the middle of the night, I'm not eliminating anyone from suspicion."

Tyler replayed Link's words in his mind as he drove toward home and Julie that night. They rattled around in his brain like pebbles in a tin can. They still irked him when he stopped at the Chinese restaurant at Four Corner Crossing and selected an array of delicacies.

By the time he let himself in through the condo's front door, his insides were churning at possibilities. He trusted every one of the men and women working for him, and he'd never believe anyone in his family could calculatedly murder a man. Blind to everything around him, he strode across the living room, into the kitchen, and started pulling open the takeout containers.

"Is something wrong?"

It took a moment for him to focus on the words and the sweet voice that carried them. Julie's voice. "No, nothing."

"You look…angry."

"I said, it's nothing," he growled. "Nothing I can't handle. Let's eat before this stuff gets cold."

He snatched plates out of the cupboard, silverware from a drawer, spun around and deposited them with a clatter on the kitchen table. Only then did he become aware that Julie hadn't moved from where she stood watching him in the doorway. He looked at her for the first time that evening…and frowned, puzzled by the white negligee and peignoir she wore. Silk and lace, trailing to the floor.

Why wasn't she wearing her usual comfy sleep shirt? Her hair was brushed until it shone, and the only makeup she wore was a trace of pale lipstick. She looked beautiful, dammit.

Then he remembered…this was her wedding night. His, too.

"Well?" he grumbled. "Aren't you hungry?"

"We're not eating until you calm down and tell me what's wrong," she said with a firmness that surprised him.

"Nothing's wrong."

"Bull." There was the faintest catch in her voice, but she wasn't letting him get away with his gruff silence. "You're obviously upset about something. Shutting me out won't make the problem go away. Don't you think talking about it might help?"

He groaned. "You don't understand."

She moved around the table, layers of silk shifting

around her body, allowing him tempting peeks at flesh, an intimate shadow, a rosy nipple. Stopping at his side, she stroked his beard-stubbled cheek with the back of her hand, then laid her cool fingertips against his temple as if he were a child and she was testing for a fever. "Give me a chance. Please."

If another woman had tried that with him, he'd have told her to mind her own damn business. But she was a Fortune now, too. And something in Julie's eyes made him realize she wasn't being nosy or trying to control him. She just wanted to help.

He leaned back against the kitchen counter and looked down at his folded hands in front of him. "Link has a new theory about the elevator accident. He believes that someone involved with the hospital's construction is behind what happened."

"Oh, Tyler, no." She touched his arm. The muscle beneath his shirt was rock-hard with tension.

He nodded solemnly. "Link even suggested someone in the family might have had a hand in it. But, I can't believe...still, it seems likely that it was someone who knew the site and had the technical know-how to sabotage an elevator."

"I'm sorry," she murmured. "This is terrible."

"It sounds to me as if someone asked Mike to meet him there. There was no other reason for him to be at the site so late at night. It had to have been someone he trusted, someone he'd be willing to give up his evening for."

"Or maybe *he* asked *them* to meet him," she suggested.

"I honestly can't see why." He caught her soothing fingertips and lifted them to his lips. "I must have barged in here sounding like a lunatic."

"No, just an especially grumpy bear," Julie said softly.

Tyler chuckled under his breath. "I'm not very pleasant

to be around when things go wrong. I don't like mistakes, carelessness, sloppy work, ignorance or stealing on the job. This just…just goes beyond the worst problem I could imagine.''

Her heart went out to him. Such a big, practical, capable man. He saw a problem and set out to solve it—the quicker the better. But now he was helpless, and it was killing him.

''Is there anything to be done right now? Anything you can do to help get to the truth sooner?'' Julie already knew the answer. She just wanted him to say it himself.

Tyler drew a long breath then slowly let it out between tight lips. ''I suppose not. Link is a capable investigator, according to Shane. He's found out more in just a few weeks than any of us ever suspected—even if it's not what we want to hear.''

''When you hire a man to dig a foundation or plaster a wall, do you worry about him doing the job right?''

He looked at her warily. ''No. I hire experienced workers and let them do their jobs.''

''And you've said Link is good at what he does.''

He nodded. ''I get your point.''

''If you don't like the truth when it comes out, there's nothing you can do to change it anyway,'' she said so softly that he felt comforted by the mere sound of her words, even though they represented a harsh reality.

Tyler pulled Julie close and pressed her head to his chest. ''You're right. Link has to do his job, and I have to do mine, which hasn't changed. I need to put up that hospital.'' He sighed into the wisps of hair falling across her forehead as she gazed up at him, watching his expression. ''It's just hard, you know, not being able to control something like this.''

And he was, he fully realized, a controller. He'd had to stop himself from coming down hard on foremen in the past when they disagreed with him. He had learned to trust Mike Dodd. That was one reason he felt he owed Mike something—at least justice, at least finding his killer.

He became aware of Julie's hands, moving in warm patterns across his shoulder blades and lower back, easing away tension even as he held her. Muscles and worries loosened and broke free, like small boats leaving their moorings to drift across a peaceful lake. He closed his eyes and let her calm him. Her lips brushed along his jaw, down his throat. He glided, floated. Being with her like this required no effort at all.

"That feels nice," he murmured. *Nice,* it occurred to him, was an understatement. *Nice* didn't begin to describe the pleasantly erotic tingles traveling through his body. Tyler felt himself shift beneath the zipper of his work jeans.

"Let's see what yummy things you have in here," she whispered.

His eyes popped open in shock, only to realize she was staring hungrily at the takeout containers. His mind wasn't on food, but maybe if he faked interest in a meal, later…. He reached for a plate.

"We won't need those." The subtle hint of authority in her voice surprised him. Julie scooped up the containers and two forks. "But you might pour us a couple of glasses of wine," she suggested, whisking herself and their feast off toward the bedroom.

Tyler watched her peignoir flow out behind her in a delicate white wave. Was this the same woman he'd met only a short time ago? The meek, nervous, virgin librarian? Can't be, he thought, shaking his head.

By the time he'd brought two glasses of a ruby-red Australian merlot into their bedroom, Julie had spread an extra sheet over the bed as a tablecloth and opened the food.

The aroma was delectable—ginger, herbs, savory spices. He'd ordered sweet, sticky orange chicken, shrimp in lobster sauce and Szechuan vegetables. When he picked up a morsel of chicken in its honeyed sauce, it was still warm.

"Sit," she said, patting the bed.

"Yes, ma'am." He wasn't absolutely sure he trusted this new Julie. It occurred to him that if she was testing her powers as a new wife, he'd be wise to set things straight and let her know he was still boss. But there was something so disarming, so sweet about the way she gave orders that he simply complied and felt amused.

Julie picked up a long, fat green bean and lifted it to his lips. He took it between his teeth, and, watching her smile, he chewed and leaned back on one elbow to savor the exotic, peppery flavors. As his mood mellowed another notch, his lust matched it. He wanted to seize her and make fierce love to her, but he reminded himself that she was still very inexperienced. He didn't want to frighten her and ruin this unexpectedly good thing.

Julie licked the sticky glaze from her fingertips, lowered her eyelashes and gazed up at him through them, sending him a clear message.

"I thought you wanted to eat," he said huskily.

"Eat and relax."

"I see." He fed her a plump, pink shrimp, dripping with sweet lobster sauce, and she drew one finger beneath his bottom lip, catching an errant speck of breading from his chicken. "Any specific means of relaxing come to your clever little mind?"

"Well," she said playfully, "as you can see, I'm already in the appropriate garb."

He looked down at his work clothes. As soon as he'd hit his office, he'd changed out of the tux. "I'd hate to spill something on my best jeans."

"Just what I was thinking." She sounded so exaggeratedly prim he couldn't help laughing.

"I'm not sure what you're up to, lady. But staying in this room with you...well, it's beginning to feel a little dangerous."

"Good thing we're married," she countered with the faintest wicked smile.

Maybe he was wrong. Maybe aliens hadn't stolen his meek bride and replaced her with this adorable temptress. Perhaps the way she was behaving now was part of what Julie had been all along, only her sensuality had been bottled up inside a frightened shell for so long she herself had never realized it existed.

He removed his shirt and tossed it onto the chair by the window, then stepped out of shoes and pants. On second thought he kept on his T-shirt and briefs. But when he sat on the bed beside Julie and reached in front of her for another crisp, fiery bean, she lifted the edge of his shirt to run her fingers beneath it and through the coarse hair on his chest.

Her fingertips were trembling. He smiled. It was comforting to know she wasn't as sure of herself as she pretended. Tyler met her eyes. They were dazzling. The colors in them changed so quickly he couldn't name one before it became another—hazel, green, fawn, topaz...

"Lovely," he murmured. Tender movements of her hands across his chest intensified as heat mounted low in his body. He moved her away from him just enough to tug his T-shirt off over his head. "I must have been mad to leave my bride on our wedding day." He pulled her into his arms and kissed her with a passion that rocked him.

"You had important work to do," she murmured between their briefly parted lips.

But perhaps he should have told Link that their meeting

would have to wait until the morning. Even now, just thinking about the investigation made his shoulders tighten.

As if she understood the turmoil bubbling inside him, Julie laid her cheek against Tyler's chest then kissed the muscled surface over his heart. Softly, her hands feathered across his shoulders until the knots loosened.

Damn, the woman was good for him. How had he ever stumbled on her? Was it fate? Or something spiritual that had begun to bind them together that night in the cave? He'd never believed in those sorts of things. Whatever the reason, she was here with him now, and, miraculously, he had the right to sleep with her every night for as long as they both lived.

Did it matter that he didn't love her or that she didn't love him? He'd begun this venture with the sure knowledge that love would never be a factor in their relationship. He'd had crushes on girls in high school and college. Had a few steamy, fleeting affairs. But he knew he'd never been in love.

If he and Julie were very lucky, they'd have fun together, share some spectacular sex...then cool down and learn to tolerate each other for the long run. Five years from now they would probably be living their own lives, speaking only when necessary to relay information about their children or pass along phone messages. But he would remain faithful to her because that was the honorable thing to do. He would always have his needs. He supposed she'd have her own. But he'd never expected more than a practical arrangement where sex was concerned. They'd both be disappointed if they expected more.

Her kisses fell across his chest, to his abdomen. His stomach twitched then tightened with anticipation of each light touch of her lips. Lower. Then lower. Until she had to kneel.

"You can't know what you're doing to a man when you tease that way," he ground out, stroking her hair as she kissed the furred flesh just above the band of his briefs, then beneath its edge.

"I have a pretty good idea." She grinned up at him, looking increasingly confident the stronger his reaction.

Yes, he was aroused. Yes, he wanted to beg her to make love to him with that delicious mouth of hers. He ached to feel her lips close around him and slide his entire length, and bring him to sweet, blazing ecstasy. But as inexperienced as she was, he still feared shocking her. He'd have to be satisfied with whatever she could handle. He would bury himself in her and whisper in her ear how beautiful she was on this their wedding night, and be thankful for that much.

He was wrenched out of his thoughts by the petal-soft motion of her hand slipping inside his briefs, stroking him. He looked down to see her bow her head toward him.

"No!" The word came out as a husky bark. "You can't...I don't want you to do anything that will..."

"Will what, Tyler?" Her eyes were sparkling.

She was being too damn playful. How could he protect her and take things slowly when she'd turned herself into this damn nymph? "You don't have to do anything that embarrasses you, just to please me."

"I won't," she promised him, and dropped a quick kiss on his tip.

Molten fire poured through his loins. In her innocence, she could have no idea what making love to him with her sweet mouth would do to him. He wanted to be gentle with her. He respected her and she deserved no less as his wife than she had before the marriage ceremony. But she was making it difficult for him to do the right thing.

Tyler sat up quickly. Twisting around onto his knees, he easily flipped Julie back onto the soft bed, hauled up layers of white silk and lace, and flung them above her waist. "Do you want me to show you what that feels like to a man?" It was the only way he could think of to delay her dangerous game just long enough for her to come to her senses. He fully expected her to back down.

She stared up at him trustingly, but said nothing.

His expert fingers quickly found the center of her womanhood. He watched her eyes widen and glaze over as he pressed two fingers into the silky, honey-drenched folds. She arched her back, tightened around him, let out a low dulcet moan.

He softly stroked her, bringing more dewy moisture. Her eyes widened still further. Her lips trembled but no words came out.

"Say something so I'll know what you're thinking," he whispered urgently.

"Yes, show me," she gasped. "Please."

Tyler slid his body down to touch his lips to the top of her thigh. Then he kissed the other before centering himself and nuzzling between them.

Julie's hands immediately clamped over his head. He froze, waiting to see if she'd push him away. Her fingers tangled through his hair, gripped him, held him to her. "Please," she whispered throatily. "Don't...don't stop." She opened herself to him.

Gently, he drew the very tip of his tongue across her, and she shuddered. He flicked his tongue over her again and again, tasting the luscious nectar that told him she was already riding a wave that would carry her over mountains. No longer hesitating, he seized her hips to bring himself still deeper, until she writhed and cried out in shocked delight.

Even when Tyler believed she'd had enough and tried to pull away, she reached out for him. But he could wait no longer. He brought himself up even with her on the bed, entered her swiftly and held her through the wild swells of her passion as she climaxed again and again, her body straining and releasing beneath him.

He was only moments behind her. He lost himself in a powerful burst within her, matching his own pleasure to hers. Then all he could do was lie over her, shuddering, amazed at what they were capable of, together.

Now woman, he thought, *you understand.*

Nine

It seemed to Julie that her days had never been sunnier. Although she still feared she would never live up to the challenge of being a Fortune, she was grateful to be one. She gloried in new freedoms—to buy herself a chic dress if the whim struck her, splurge on a massage at the spa or purchase a gourmet sauté pan to use in preparing meals for Tyler and herself. She felt useful, knowing she could take care of Tyler and make a nice home for him.

He had given her a charge card and told her to purchase whatever she needed for herself and the house. Julie wasn't frivolous, but delighted in the notion that she could buy literally anything she liked in all of Pueblo. Even stopping for a frozen yogurt without counting pennies out of the bottom of her purse seemed a small and appreciated extravagance. She savored her new life to its fullest, but she still didn't trust it.

Tyler made love to her nearly every night, whisking her

away from reality into a world of sensations so achingly beautiful she longed to find more ways to please him in return. She had no doubt that she was in love with him. But she dared not tell him. Hadn't they made a pact at the very beginning? He never uttered the word *love* to her while they caressed each other, although he whispered other tender phrases or sometimes called out her name at the height of his ecstasy.

But about ten days after their wedding, a subtle change came about. Tyler seemed distracted when they made love, and began to spend less time at the condo. He rarely smiled, and she sensed his mind was far away from her.

"Is something wrong?" she asked him one morning before he left for the site.

"Nothing I can't handle," he returned evasively, his gray eyes so dark they approached black.

She sighed as she watched him leave, wishing she knew if his moodiness was due to more complications with the hospital's construction, another worrisome turn in the murder investigation, or something she'd done to displease him. Perhaps, she mused sadly, this is to be the natural course of our relationship; already he had grown bored with her. A voice within her warned that their days together were numbered, and this saddened her beyond all the loneliness she'd suffered in the past.

He was her husband, her missing half. It was impossible to share meals, a home and a bed with the man and keep her emotional distance. How long she could stay in Pueblo and watch him slip further and further away from her, she didn't know.

Tyler met with his crew chiefs each morning and briefed them on the jobs that needed most urgently to be completed. From one day to the next, work moved along at the hospital site, but never fast enough for him. He blamed Julie for this.

He felt driven to finish his work, hurry home to Julie and fall into her soft arms. He yearned to sit with her and share a quiet, satisfying meal and a mellow glass of wine. He wanted to be anywhere with her rather than at the site or his office. He'd never put anything ahead of his work, and the drastic change troubled him.

His marriage was meant to be the solution to a problem...not a problem in itself. Yes, his inheritance was secure now, but he faced an emotional maze he found impossible to negotiate. One moment he felt confused, angry and resentful of Julie's sudden intrusion in his life. The next he was overwhelmed by gratitude, affection and a physical need for her so intense it terrified him. He knew he'd have to sort out his feelings for her and come to terms with their marriage in some way. But that would have to wait until the hospital was finished and the investigation resolved.

Each day, Tyler fought the urge to dash home to Julie by forcing himself to work further into the evening. He plowed through paperwork, contracts, deadlines. Was this love? He could no longer swear that such an emotion didn't exist, or that he was immune to it. Worse yet, he feared that if he ever confessed his true feelings to Julie, he'd be lost. If he loved her and she didn't return his love, there would be nothing to hold her to him. Money obviously held no power over her. She would simply walk out of his life, leaving him a broken man.

One evening, Tyler met his cousin Shane at the Camel Corral. The interior of the popular Pueblo restaurant was dark and masculine—wood paneling permeated with the aroma of thousands of steaks charbroiled over the years; a huge stone fireplace and richly patterned mosaic tile floors.

"Sorry I had to keep you from going straight home to Julie," Shane said as he took a long, smooth swallow of beer from an icy mug. "Thought I'd better meet with you to discuss an interview I'll be giving to the press. I need to know what I can or can't say if they ask about the investigation."

Tyler nodded. "Good idea. What kind of interview is this?" Shane had a medical practice in Pueblo but was also the family's expert on Native American culture.

"With my sister Isabelle officially engaged to Brad Rowan, it looks as if we'll soon be able to reclaim Lightfoot's Plateau."

"Any idea when the transfer of the deed will take place? It would make sense to start taking bids on the restoration of the cave drawings as soon as possible, given the rate of deterioration."

"No date yet, but I'm going to call a press conference and fill in the local media on the history of the Papago people, who are now called the Tohono O'odham, and the cultural importance of the plateau. I want the public to know how important it will be to our people still living in this area when the land is actually turned over to us."

"You might want to brief Rowan, too," Tyler mused. "Last time I talked with him, he seemed to assume we would be developing the site to bring in tourists. I don't think he realizes that if we do decide to let tourists into the cave, any profit from admission fees will go to helping the children of the tribe."

"Right."

"About the investigation," Tyler said, getting to the point of their meeting. "I think you'd better check with Link Templeton to see how much information he's turned over to the police." He filled his cousin in on his most recent conversation with Link.

When Tyler finished, Shane stared at him from across the booth where they sat. "Unbelievable. He actually thinks one of us did it?"

"I'm not sure what he thinks. He just told me he wasn't ready to eliminate anyone from suspicion. And it won't do this project any good to become involved in a scandal."

"Enough said. I think I'll just defer all questions to Link and let him handle them. He seems to think fast on his feet."

"Good idea," Tyler agreed.

"So how's it going with your new bride?" Shane asked as he finished off his beer.

It took Tyler a moment to adjust to the new topic. "Great," he answered at last.

Shane studied his expression. "Julie seems a real fine woman."

"She is." Tyler smiled weakly. "She's the best."

"But?"

Tyler looked up sharply. "What do you mean?"

"Jason told me an incredible tall tale about you picking her out of a dating service catalogue." Shane was studying him with an amused expression.

"He always was one for a good joke," Tyler muttered, thinking dark thoughts that included stringing up his brother from the nearest tree.

Shane didn't look convinced. "However you two met, it seems a match made in heaven."

Tyler shrugged. "That's what I'm worried about." He chugged down three fast swallows of warm suds while Shane scowled at him.

Maybe it would help to talk to someone. He could trust his cousin, unlike Jason, to keep a secret if necessary.

After hearing the details, Shane summed up the situation. "So now you're married, and you don't know what to do about it."

"Exactly. I guess I'm just trying to figure out what to do with my feelings for her. I thought I could handle it all real easy. You know, fulfill the terms of the contract. Treat her like another building project. It was supposed to be a business proposition. Clean and simple."

"But it's become more than that," Shane guessed.

"A hell of a lot more." Tyler shook his head.

His cousin grinned at him and spun his empty mug between two hands on the dark wooden tabletop. "Sounds like you've taken the big leap into love without realizing you were doing it."

"Not love!" Tyler objected, then saw the skepticism in Shane's eyes. "At least, I don't think it is. What it is...I can't put my finger on." He groaned and glared at the bottom of his own mug, wondering where the beer had gone.

"A long time ago, it almost happened to me." Shane's voice was distant, wistful.

Tyler looked up. "Love, you mean?"

"Maybe. I didn't wait around long enough to find out. Remember my college girlfriend, Cynthia McCree?"

"The grad student—criminology, bound for law school. Blonde...blue eyes?"

"That's the one. We had a fast and furious affair."

"Her choice or yours?"

"Mine. I panicked. I thought I was falling in love with her, and I couldn't handle it. I just walked out of her life."

Tyler thought of all the women he could have fallen in love with, but hadn't.

"Do you regret leaving her?" he asked.

"I think about her sometimes. I wonder what might

have happened to her since then, and what might have happened to us if we'd stayed together."

"You're saying you wish you'd given marriage a shot?"

"Maybe. I could at least have given our relationship my honest best." He looked at Tyler. "It might have been worth the risk, to have a good woman at my side and the possibility of a family of my own."

"I keep coming back to one thing, though. My father."

Shane folded his large hands on the table. "Why him?"

"I don't know why I should be any better at handling marriage and raising a family."

"He does okay by you guys."

"Now, sure. But when I was a kid…it wasn't easy. He was too busy building a struggling construction business to spend time with his children. If I have kids, I want it to be different."

"Maybe just being aware of the problem is enough," Shane mused. "That way you can do something about it."

Tyler shook his head wearily. All well and good to say it, but was he up to the challenge? Could he ever let go of the business enough to let Julie and their children into his life in a way that really counted? "I just don't know."

"Hey!" a familiar voice greeted them from across the room. Jason wove between tables, spun a chair and straddled the seat. "I've been hunting all over town for you." He looked at Tyler. "Called your place. Julie said she didn't know where you were."

Tyler winced. Already he was doing a lousy job of being a husband. "What's up?"

"I was driving past the site, and I thought I saw someone walking around inside the security fence. I stopped to get a better look. It was Brad Rowan."

Shane caught Tyler's eye. "Rowan has no reason for lurking around the site at this hour. Does he?"

"Hell, no," Tyler snorted. "I mean, his family supplies a good deal of our building materials, but that doesn't give him twenty-four-hour access to the project." He shot to his feet. "Are you sure it was him?"

Jason hesitated. "Looked like him. Where're you going?"

"Down there to see what's going on." Tyler tossed a twenty down on the table. It would more than cover their tab. "More likely it's a local scavenging for tools. I don't want to go down there tomorrow morning and find things missing."

"Wait." Jason stopped him with a firm hand on his arm. He glanced at Shane quickly for support. "We're going with you. Until Templeton gets to the bottom of what happened to Mike none of us should be over there alone."

"Fine," Tyler snapped. "Let's go."

An hour later, Tyler quietly let himself into the condo. Julie had left a light on for him in the living room. He turned it off on his way through and undressed quietly in the bathroom so as not to wake her.

Although he, Shane and Jason had searched the site with the help of the security guard, they'd found no intruders and nothing appeared to be out of order or missing. One more complication, Tyler thought grimly. Was this how it had been for his father? Had there always been another emergency that kept Devlin from his wife and sons?

Tyler felt a cool, gray sadness closing in on him. Maybe there was no way to change his workaholic nature or the way the business worked. Maybe being a good father wasn't something a man could simply decide to do.

He slipped into bed with Julie, careful not to jostle her.

Her back was turned to him, and he slid close, curving himself around the soft swell of her bottom, feeling her warmth sink into his body, and, as exhausted as he was, slowly arouse him. He could make love to her right now, even as she was waking to his touch, before she was fully aware of what was happening. The thought excited him.

But, he told himself, he'd be a cad if he took her like that now. He'd barely looked her way in days. He'd been so troubled, thinking about them, he had avoided real intimacy.

Gently, he draped his arm around her silken shoulders and buried his nose in the shampoo-fragrant fluff of warm brown hair at the back of her neck. He held her like a secret. A secret he didn't even dare whisper to himself.

Still in her robe, Julie listlessly puttered around the kitchen for a few minutes then made herself a cup of tea while Tyler finished showering and shaving before work. She curled up in his favorite overstuffed armchair by the front window and gazed out over the dawn-streaked desert. Her head felt foggy from too-shallow sleep, her heart as heavy as the stone walls of the Papago cave.

Julie turned at the sound of Tyler's footsteps crossing the living room. *He is beautiful,* she thought, mesmerized by his lean blue-jeans-clad form. When he saw her in the chair, he stopped, and, for a heartbeat, she was sure he was going to say something important.

But the moment passed, and he lowered his eyes and grumbled, "Forgot something."

She watched him disappear into the den then come out again with a folder of papers. He stopped in front of her and stared down with a disapproving frown. "You look tired. Why don't you go back to bed?"

She gazed up at him sadly. "I couldn't sleep."

"Any particular reason?"

She sighed. Shrugged. What good would it do to explain? Admitting to him that she'd fallen in love with him—contrary to the ground rules they'd set up for their relationship—would do neither of them any good. "No, just restless I suppose."

He studied her for a long moment, then mumbled something about the time of the month and took himself off for what she knew would be another very long day.

For another ten minutes Julie sat numbly staring out at the new spring day that promised to be warm and sweet despite her somber mood. At last, his words sank in, and she realized they might offer a partial explanation for her inability to shake off her depression. The days and nights since she'd come to Pueblo had been so busy, demanding all her attention, that she'd totally lost track of the underlying rhythms of her life. Wasn't it close to time for her period? She was never late. Not even a day. Her feminine cycles were as dependable as the moon's. And yet...

She pushed herself out of the chair, found her purse and pulled out her checkbook with its calendar in the back. By her calculations, her period should have started six days ago. If she was pregnant, she must have conceived that very first time they'd made love, in the cave. It was unlikely but not impossible. Suddenly, everything that had seemed difficult now felt overwhelming.

Taking a deep breath, Julie gathered her courage. She couldn't just sit and feel sorry for herself. First things first. She had to find out if her suspicions were true. After a hot shower, she dressed in casual clothing and drove to the drugstore.

Fifteen minutes later, after she'd worked up the nerve to take the home pregnancy test, she stood in the bathroom staring down at the plastic strip, shocked to see what she'd already told herself might be true. She was pregnant.

For blissful seconds she felt lighter than air, happier than at any moment in her life, tingling with life. Her dream had come true! She was going to be a mother! Her family was on its way!

Just as suddenly, she fell to earth. Now she had no choice but to deal with reality. The father of her baby did not and never would love her. What was she going to do?

Julie thought again about talking to Kate. She was so wise, so understanding of the ways of the heart. But to admit to Kate that she'd married her grandson for his sperm and his income, that was something she couldn't do. She felt utterly ashamed.

With bitter resolve, she picked up the phone and called the branch library in Houston. Luckily, they hadn't hired a replacement yet. A second call confirmed that her old apartment had been leased to another couple, who would move in the following month. But an efficiency was available in the same complex and she could transfer her things from one to the other quite easily.

Plans whirred through her mind. Money would be difficult, because she wouldn't ask for child support from Tyler after welching on their deal. As for Tyler, he'd be just fine without her underfoot, she told herself. His parents would blame her for the breakup, knowing that Tyler had married her and provided a home for her all in good faith. He should be able to keep his inheritance; Kate would argue his case if Devlin threatened to take it from him. And they'd each have what they'd originally wanted. Wasn't that enough?

Frantically, she pushed aside the answer she hadn't wanted to hear. *No, it's not enough. Not anymore!*

Julie's heart raced as she threw clothes into the suitcase

she'd brought with her the day she'd come to Pueblo. Tears clinging to her eyelashes, she looked one last time at the closet full of beautiful clothes Kate had bought for her. It wouldn't be right to take them with her. It would be like stealing. The dresses, wedding gifts, Tyler's lovely rings, things she'd lovingly purchased for the condo… she'd take none of them. She already felt like a thief, carrying Tyler's baby away from him.

An hour later, after many false starts, she finished her farewell note to Tyler and laid it on the kitchen table where they'd shared the most beautiful meals of her life. She slid a corner of it under the bowl of fresh flowers she'd bought the day before, so it wouldn't blow off the table when he walked past. Tenderly, she touched her fingertips to the small lavender square of paper, as if blessing it, then picked up her suitcase and left.

As Julie drove east, through Tucson then along I-10 toward the snow-crested Rincon Mountains, heading back toward Houston and her old life…she thought of a man as magnificent in his own way as the mountains of Arizona. A man she would never forget. The only man she'd ever loved, or likely ever would.

Tyler didn't leave the trailer at the construction site until nearly eight o'clock that night. All day long he'd thought of Julie, trying to put his feelings for her into words for himself, so that he could explain them to her. But his emotions were a hopeless muddle.

Did he love her? No, the real question was, did he *dare* to love her? Because once he admitted that much, she had the power to destroy him.

But when he got home, he discovered her car wasn't there. Just as well, he thought. Now he'd have a little more time to get his head together. They had to talk tonight. He couldn't let things go on as they had been.

Tyler checked the kitchen to see what she'd prepared for him, but no plate piled with tasty food awaited him. He scowled, sensing something wasn't right. The answering machine. If she was delayed somewhere in town, she would call. He dashed across the living room, into his study. The red light on the machine was blinking. He punched the play button and waited anxiously for the tape to rewind.

"Julie, call me if you want to come with me to the spa. I'm leaving in half an hour, dear." It was Kate, sounding bouncy and ready for fun.

He smiled. Had his grandmother commandeered his wife for the entire day?

The next message began: "Julie, please give me a call when you get in. I have yet another delivery of tardy wedding gifts." Jasmine's voice hesitated. "And even if you don't want to pick them up today, ring us anyway. Kate hasn't heard back from you. She's pouting."

His Julie certainly had made inroads on his family. He'd never dreamed any woman he brought home to them would be so eagerly or quickly accepted.

The final message played back: "Julie—" Kate again "—it's nearly 7:00 p.m. I'm worried about you, dear. I'll feel like an old fool if you just took the day to drive into Tucson to shop. But I thought you told me you would be available to do something today. Just let me know you're all right, dear."

Tyler's amusement vanished. How thoughtless could she be? Julie had been away from the house all day without telling anyone where she'd be. She didn't have an obligation to inform the family of everything she did, but at least she could have left a note for him!

Two hours later, she still hadn't shown up. Tyler was no longer angry. He was frantic. When the kitchen phone rang, he dove for it. "Where the hell are you?" he barked into it.

"Tyler?"

"Oh. Hi, Mom. Sorry 'bout that." He smacked the heel of his hand against his forehead.

"Julie's not home yet?"

"No, I'm sorry she hasn't returned your and Kate's calls."

"Don't worry about us, we're fine. Sterling has returned from his business trip and wants to meet your new bride."

"Well, if I could find *my new bride,* I'd be glad to introduce them."

"Tyler?" Jasmine asked. "Is everything all right? I mean, Julie's happy here, isn't she?"

"Of course she's happy. How could any woman not be happy under the circumstances?"

"Oh, Tyler." She sighed.

"What?" She'd better not blame him! He hadn't done anything wrong.

"Sometimes you're so into your own world, you can't see into anyone else's."

He walked with the receiver to the table and sat down, resigned to a lecture. But his elbow hit the flower bowl and water spilled over its edge, creating a little lake.

Apparently, Jasmine was too busy scolding him to hear him swearing. He reached for the sponge beside the sink. Clamping the phone between his chin and shoulder, he lifted the bowl and started mopping up water. His glance settled on a small square of paper. As he read the words Julie had written, his mother's voice faded into the background and water dribbled unnoticed off the table edge onto the floor.

Tyler, I'm sorry. I thought I could do this, but I can't go on pretending we're something we never can be. Please forgive me for any inconvenience I may have caused you. Tell your family whatever you like. They're good people; I didn't mean to hurt them.

Love, Julie

P.S. The rings are on your night table.

"Mother, I know where she is," he said tightly. "You can stop worrying about her. It seems she can take care of herself." He quickly promised to explain later then hung up.

Crushing the letter in his fist, Tyler let out a howl of rage. He slammed his fist down on the table. Pain shot through his knuckles and up his arm. He raced into the bedroom. There, beside the lamp where she'd said they'd be, were the diamond solitaire and gold wedding band they'd picked out together. He swept them off the table with the back of his hand and heard them clatter against the wall. Where they landed he didn't bother to notice.

To hell with Julie Parker.

Ten

Her first day back in Houston was the hardest, but Julie managed to keep so busy she was too exhausted to dwell on all she'd left behind in Pueblo. She moved her things out of her old one-bedroom, into the even smaller efficiency. She dropped off the rental car and paid for the mileage and an extra fee for its return to another city. She filled out the necessary paperwork for her re-employment and made an appointment with an obstetrician.

Above all, she concentrated on thoughts that were hopeful, if not exactly happy. In a little more than eight short months, the doctor confirmed, she'd be a mother. She and her baby would be together.

Another good thought struck her a few days later. Since she had been back in Houston, people treated her differently. They seemed friendlier, more interested in her. She decided this might have less to do with them and more with her. She felt confident in everything she did. No

longer did she avoid strangers. She listened more closely
to what people had to say and expressed opinions of her
own. She walked two miles every morning for exercise,
and felt more in tune with her body. Her short stay with
the outgoing Fortunes seemed to have had an interesting
effect on her. There was so much to experience of life,
and she wanted to taste it all!

Julie vowed she would pass this enthusiasm along to her
baby. Her child wouldn't grow up a victim, afraid of his
own shadow. The child she and Tyler had made together
would love life, reach out for it and welcome challenge.

Unfortunately, she would never be able to thank Tyler
for what he'd done for her. And she'd never show him the
child they'd created, because he might try to take her baby
from her. Not for himself, for his family. His powerful
family who clung together through triumphs and tragedies.
He would want her child even if he no longer wanted her.

Now, four days after leaving Pueblo, she sat in her tiny
kitchen and buried her face in her hands but this time did
not weep. The thought of Tyler would always bring sadness, because she had loved the man so completely and
would never see him again. But the memories were nearly
all sweet. And the gifts he'd given her—their child, her
knowledge of herself as a woman and her courage to face
life head-on—would remain hers forever.

Gradually, Julie became aware of a distant commotion.
It sounded as if someone was knocking down walls with
a battering ram. Was the maintenance man getting an early
start? She glanced at the wall-clock. A very early start. It
was only 7:00 a.m., and a Saturday. The man was putting
himself at risk.

By the time she finished washing and dressing, the noise
outside had grown even louder. Now she could hear angry
shouts. She lifted the chintz curtain across the only win-

dow on the front side of her apartment and saw a figure, fist raised over his head, pounding on a door. When it opened, he said a few words to the person inside, then immediately moved on to the next door and pounded again.

What on earth was he doing? Selling something? And with such a belligerent attitude!

She stood transfixed, watching him work his way down the row of apartments. He was tall, wore jeans and a plaid shirt. A black Stetson hid his face. He moved to the next door, and she could feel anger in his fast, powerful strides. He was a man determined to do what he'd come for. Her heart quivered with recognition. Pools of perspiration collected in her palms.

No, she thought. *Please, don't let it be him!*

He reached the apartment of a retired woman Julie had known for years. The man spoke briefly to her, then turned and looked straight toward her apartment. He poked the brim of his hat up off his forehead with the knuckles of one hand. Hard gray eyes glared her way. Eyes that had seduced her, darker than a wet night. The face of a warring brave gleamed in the early sunlight.

"Oh, no!" she gasped, falling back from the window. Why had he come after her? She could think of only one reason.

Julie grabbed her purse and keys, and started for her back door. But he was already hammering at her front door and neighbors were shouting at him to stop. His fists rained down brutally on her door.

"Julie, I know you're in there. Open up!"

"Go away, Tyler!"

The knocking stopped; she stepped cautiously toward the door. Had he left, just like that? No, she could hear his rasping breath on the other side. "Julie. Let me in."

He was no longer shouting. His mouth must have been inches from her door; his voice penetrated the metal panel easily. "I swear, if you don't, I'll break down this door. You know I can do it."

Yes, she knew. He was strong. And if he couldn't do it with his bare hands and muscled shoulders, he'd no doubt produce a bulldozer and take out half her kitchen wall with it.

"Hold on," she said, reaching over to turn the dead bolt. Her one safeguard was that everyone in the neighborhood had heard him, and, without doubt, someone had already called the police to complain. She cracked the door and peered out at him.

He didn't wait for her to open it the rest of the way or ask him in. His forearm hit the surface and swung it wide. It was all she could do to jump out of his way before he tramped over her. He slammed the door behind him. "What the hell do you think you're doing?" he bellowed.

She planted her feet in the middle of the room and stood her ground. "I was getting ready to go to work."

"Don't give me that—"

"Tyler, I left you a note. Didn't you get it?"

"I got your goddamn note!" he bellowed, towering over her. "What makes you think you can walk out on me like that?"

"It wasn't going to work," she said flatly.

"Why not?"

"Because..." She blinked up at him. His face was a mask of pure rage. She'd never seen him like this. It was terrifying. "Because I couldn't pretend to your family that I was something I wasn't."

"That's not why you left," he growled. His hands shot out and closed around her arms before she could move out of range.

She let out an involuntary whimper, but her curiosity got the better of her fear. "Why do you think I left?"

"You played me like a pro, didn't you? You told me you weren't interested in anything but a baby. And the ironic thing is, you were telling the truth. As soon as you'd got what you came for—you ran back home."

She opened her mouth to deny it, to cry out to him that she'd never intended to hurt him...but she couldn't force a word of any kind between her stiff lips.

He stormed on. "I found the pregnancy test in the bathroom wastebasket two days after you left. You didn't do a very good job of hiding it, Julie."

In truth, she hadn't tried to hide it. That hadn't occurred to her. She wondered now if she might have subconsciously wanted Tyler to know he was going to be a father. But did that make any sense when she'd run from him?

She shrugged hopelessly. "I'm sorry," she whispered even as his fingers bit more fiercely into her arms.

He shook her hard enough to make her head wobble. "Damn you, Julie. I've met a lot of women, but none as coldly calculating as you. You had everyone fooled."

Tears gathered in her eyes, and she couldn't wipe them away while he had her pinned. "N-n-n-no," she sobbed. "I didn't try to fool—"

"If you think I'll let you take my child away, you manipulative witch—"

"You didn't want a baby! That was your family's idea." She stared up at him in shock. "You didn't even want a wife. How can you be so upset now that you won't have either?"

He wasn't listening to her. "I can make you come back to Pueblo and stay there until the baby is born. Legally, I could pull it off. And afterward, I could take you to court for custody of my child."

She broke free of his grip and staggered backward before running into the dishwasher. "You wouldn't."

"The Fortunes have very good lawyers," he stated coldly.

Her eyes narrowed. "And they'll have one hell of a fight on their hands."

Something flashed across his features. A momentary look of admiration. Or excitement? But it was gone before she could label it. Then he was frowning at her, more puzzled than angry but holding his fury in reserve should she say the wrong thing.

Julie sighed. "Tyler, I won't lie to you. I couldn't bear to stay in Pueblo. I know I promised to marry you if you'd give me a child. And now you've kept your part of the bargain. But I hadn't counted on—"

"On what? On getting pregnant so soon?" he said sullenly. "You thought you'd be hanging around for a few months or even a year or two before you got your wish?"

"No," she said sadly, "although I had hoped I'd be able to stay...for a long time."

His scowl deepened. "What are you trying to say?"

Outside car doors shut quietly. Footsteps moved stealthily along the sidewalk between apartments. Julie pushed the interruption from her mind and concentrated on what she had to say to the man who had won her heart then broken it.

"I thought I could be like you," she whispered. "I thought I could treat our relationship like a business. Go through the motions. Enjoy the advantages of being a Fortune and even allow myself the physical pleasures of sleeping with you, without feeling anything for you. I was wrong. I fell in love with you, Tyler."

She looked up at him. His face was a stony blank. "You

left because you fell in love with me," he repeated woodenly.

A sound near her door made her glance that way for just an instant. Then she looked back at Tyler. "How could I stay?" she asked. "I couldn't live in the same town with you, in the same house, knowing you felt nothing for me. I was hurting, Tyler. Don't you see it could only get worse? I'm sorry. I tried. I just can't do it."

A look of amazement slowly lightened his eyes. He started to speak, but his words were drowned out by a booming voice from the other side of the door.

"Police! Open the door."

Julie stared numbly at her poor, battered door.

"Ma'am, are you all right? Your neighbors said a man busted into your apartment. Ma'am, please open the door if you can."

Tyler opened the door for her. Two uniformed Houston police officers burst into the room, weapons drawn. Tyler rolled his eyes. "Thank goodness for neighbors."

Julie stared at him, more interested in the words she'd missed than the presence of the law in her home. "What did you just say?"

"Ma'am, are you all right?" one of the officers persisted. "Do you know this man?"

"I thought I did," she said softly, not taking her eyes from Tyler. "What were you just saying?"

"I said, I love you, Julie."

Her heart tripped over its own beat. "You're just saying that to make me go back with you. Because of the baby."

The cops looked at each other.

"No," he said. "I'm telling you I love you because it's true. Shane said something to me the night you left. It should have made me realize right then how I felt about

you. Instead, it took a couple of days to sink in. I've loved
you since the first moment I saw you in that crazy video.''

Now the two officers really looked interested.

Julie ignored them and stepped closer to Tyler. ''Is this
true?''

He brought her into his arms. ''I knew there was something special about you that first time I saw you. I just
didn't know what to call it. And when you came to Pueblo
to check me out, I sensed you belonged there. You felt
right in my house, and in my arms.''

One of the cops grumbled something to his partner, and
they both holstered their guns.

''Lady, next time you have a fight with your boyfriend,
at least tell him where you are so he doesn't terrorize the
entire county trying to find you.''

Julie smiled and mouthed the word *sorry* against Tyler's
chest. They left, and she could hear them reassuring her
neighbors that everything was under control.

''Tyler, please don't tease me. I need the truth, not a
fairy tale to make me feel better. If you don't love me, tell
me. Now that I know the baby is important to you, we'll
work things out somehow.''

He touched his lips to hers. ''Have I ever told you anything but the truth?''

''No,'' she whispered.

He kissed her lightly again. ''I can't tell you how I hurt
inside when you left me. It wasn't until you were gone
that I knew my own heart. But I couldn't come after you
then, because I didn't believe you would ever love me in
return. When we struck our agreement, all you wanted was
a child. I thought that was still all that mattered to you. I
wasn't about to go begging.''

''Oh, Tyler. I'm so very sorry. It was because I loved

you so much that I had to leave. You were so distant, I couldn't get through to you.''

He pressed her head to his chest and she felt his heart beating. This is where I belong, she thought. With this man I love, who loves me.

''I thought I didn't want to be a father,'' he tried to explain, ''because I believed I'd be a lousy one. Last night I talked to Jason about how it has been for him with his daughter. If he can do it with Lisa, I can find a way to be a good father to our children. I promise. But I also want to be your husband. During the short time we were together, I learned to appreciate all a good woman could do to make my life meaningful. You're that good woman, Julie.''

Then he held her tight and kissed her till her head spun. And she knew in her heart that as long as Tyler Fortune lived, she'd never see another lonely or loveless day.

It was the end of March, and spring bloomed vigorously across the desert. Tyler split most of his days between Fortune Construction headquarters and the hospital, but when he came home he shared with Julie the triumphs and setbacks of the day. She liked that the project meant so much to Tyler. He cared about his heritage, cared about children and families. These were good signs. A man so honorable, who felt so deeply that these things were important…he deserved to be loved.

One night as they lay in bed, holding hands after making love, Julie told him about a hospital back in Houston that had a wonderful in-house learning center for young patients. Tyler listened quietly to her description of the tutoring program for long-term residents and the library in the play center.

''I think I know a way we can incorporate something

similar into the design of our hospital," he said slowly. His thumb circled softly over the pulsepoint in her wrist, moving a little faster as he grew more excited over her idea. "Would you be willing to meet with my architects to discuss redesigning the floor plan of one of the wings?"

Julie was thrilled. "I'd love to. And if you like I can draw up a list of books to order for the children's library, and learning materials for the tutors to use with your patients." She bubbled on excitedly. "All you'll need is one full-time paid teacher. The other tutors can be volunteers. That's something I'd love to do myself if—"

He stilled her lips with a kiss. "I have a feeling you're already a Fortune at heart. If we can just get this hospital built, it will be a second home to you."

"Yes," she said, knowing he was right. And that night when she fell asleep in his strong arms, she dreamed of all she could do to help children in need, while she raised her own precious tribe with Tyler.

Tyler woke Julie one Saturday morning with a soft kiss on her forehead. "Get dressed," he whispered. "I have something to show you. Meet you out at the truck."

He waited while she found a pair of jeans that still nearly fit over her expanding belly and climbed sleepily into the truck beside him. He handed her a steaming mug of coffee. Just the way she liked it—two sugars, lots of cream.

She took a sip then snuggled up to him. "What's up?"

"We're going on a picnic."

"For breakfast?"

They drove toward the edge of town then out across the desert. It wasn't long before he could tell she thought she knew where they were headed. He smiled to himself, enjoying the last few minutes of his secret.

"Has the restoration begun at the plateau?" she asked.

"That will have to wait until the property officially changes hands."

He slanted her a look. She seemed surprised when they rounded Lightfoot's Plateau and continued on for another few miles. The land began to rise into foothills covered with scrub brush and a few stunted trees. It was dramatically rough and beautiful land, and she often told him how much it suited him. He pulled the truck off the road, got out and took a basket from the rear bed. Opening her door, he offered her a hand down.

Julie jumped to the ground and looked around with an adorable pout. "What is this place?"

"Ours," he said.

She stared at him. "You own this land?"

He nodded as he spread a blanket on a flat patch of land sheltered on three sides by the rocky hillside. Protected from the desert heat by the shadow of the mountains, wild roses, gum plants and sheep sorrel blossomed. The open side looked out over the valley with Lightfoot's Plateau rising in the middle. An early-morning sun cast golden shadows across the land and stately saguaro cacti, blooming in brilliant pinks and oranges.

"It's magnificent," Julie breathed, sitting down on the blanket.

"I'm glad you like it because, after the hospital is finished, I want to build us a house on this spot." He watched her expression shift from surprise to delight.

"Oh, Tyler!" She grabbed him around both legs and hugged so hard he lost his balance and tumbled, laughing, onto the blanket beside her. "You've already given me so much! I can't imagine a better place for us to live and raise our children." She kissed him happily on the mouth then reached inside the basket and pulled out a container of freshly cut melon. "I suppose the least I can do is feed you."

Tyler took the plastic bowl from her and laid it aside. "First, I think we should christen our home site."

Julie's eyes gleamed with anticipation of his touch. "Will it be very long before we can make love in our new house?"

A cloud passed briefly over his joy. "I hope not." He touched her cheek tenderly then traced her sweet lips with one finger. "That will depend upon what the police and Link are able to uncover in the next few months. Until then, do you think our little condo and here, under the Arizona skies, will do?"

She grinned up at him. "It will do very nicely," she whispered. "Now kiss me…as if you love me more than life itself."

And he did.

*   *   *   *   *

FORTUNE FAMILY TREE: THE ARIZONA BRANCH

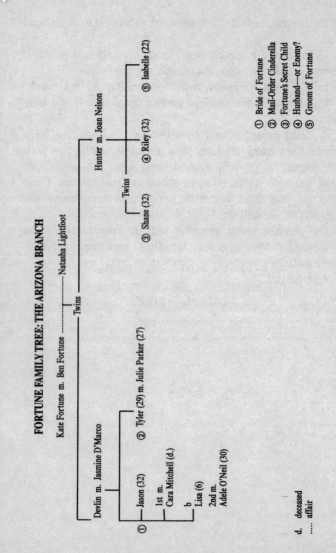

Kate Fortune m. Ben Fortune ········· Natasha Lightfoot

Twins

Devlin m. Jasmine D'Marco

① Jason (32)   ② Tyler (29) m. Julie Parker (27)

1st m.
Cara Mitchell (d.)

b

Lisa (6)

2nd m.
Adele O'Neil (30)

Hunter m. Joan Nelson

Twins

③ Shane (32)   ④ Riley (32)   ⑤ Isabelle (22)

① Bride of Fortune
② Mail-Order Cinderella
③ Fortune's Secret Child
④ Husband—or Enemy?
⑤ Groom of Fortune

d. deceased
····· affair

Find out what happens when
Shane Fortune is reunited with
his long-ago love, Cynthia McCree, in

FORTUNE'S SECRET CHILD

coming only to Silhouette Desire
in October 2000.

For a sneak preview,
please turn the page.

One

"Just what do you think you're doing here?" Cynthia McCree said, making no effort to curb the edge of displeasure surrounding her words.

A sudden twinge of discomfort reinforced her awareness of the way she was dressed. She tightened the sash around her waist and pulled the collar of her robe around her neck. She put as much authority in her voice as she could dredge up from her rapidly dwindling inner reserve of confidence. "I made sure the doors were locked before going to bed. How did you get in here?"

As a corporate attorney she had learned to read people. She immediately recognized Shane Fortune's body language—leaning forward in an attempt to psychologically throw her off balance, the unsettling way his dark piercing eyes tried to look inside her, his attempt to control the situation and control her. It had worked back then when her worldly experience was limited to Pueblo, Arizona, but it wasn't going to work anymore. She had long since become toughened by the realities of life. She pulled her determination together, held her ground and refused to back down from his aggressive manner.

"You're asking how *I* got in?" Had Shane heard her correctly? Was she really challenging his right to be in his own house? None of this made any sense to him. He maintained his outer facade of total authority as he scrambled to put things into some kind of perspective. "I think a better question would be what are *you* doing in *my* house?" The tightness in her jaw relaxed a little. Disbelief covered her features where determination had been just a moment earlier. "How can that possibly be?"

The sharp edge that surrounded her words melted away as it turned into bewilderment. She seemed to be staring into space rather than focusing on anything. It almost sounded as if she were trying to work out a problem in her mind rather than talking to him. "Kate insisted that I stay here until I get my father's estate settled and find a job. She led me to believe that she owned this house, that it was leased to someone who was going to be out of state for a while. She certainly didn't tell me this house belonged to you."

Shane knitted his brow in frustration. He shook his head, hoping it would settle the puzzle pieces into their proper place. "Kate said you could stay in my house? Your father's estate? What's going on here?" Shane took a calming breath as he attempted to collect his thoughts. On more than one occasion over the past six years he had envisioned a reunion with Cynthia and pondered what might have been had he not cut her out of his life. The thoughts always turned to sadness, so he had refused to dwell on it. Now here she was, more beautiful than ever, the flesh-and-blood person, rather than a figment of his imagination, and he didn't know how to handle it.

He motioned for her to follow him into the kitchen. "I must be missing something. It's been a couple of weeks since I talked to Kate. I told her I would be attending a medical conference up in Phoenix. I wasn't scheduled to be home until tomorrow but decided to drive back tonight instead."

Cynthia glanced nervously toward the top of the stairs. She didn't want their conversation to wake Bobby. Things were awkward enough without her son making an unexpected appearance.

"Kate offered me this house to stay in until I could get my father's estate straightened out, find a place to live and get a job. I told Kate I would pay rent while I was here."

"That still doesn't tell me how and why you and Kate even got together."

"I don't need your permission before speaking with someone." She glared at him. "But for your information she read the obituary notice in the newspaper. It mentioned the graveside service that took place this morning." Her voice softened as thoughts and feelings from several years ago invaded her consciousness. "I was surprised to see her there. I had only met her briefly on a couple of occasions back when you and I..."

The memory of their heated passion and an intense love affair she had thought would last a lifetime brought her words to a halt.

But seeing him again now did more than just resurrect heated desires and inflamed emotions. It shoved her greatest fear to the front of the line, an all-consuming dread that nearly paralyzed her with fright. Her most closely guarded secret must be protected at all costs.

She could never allow Shane Fortune to know that he was the father of her son.

FORTUNE'S Children™

*The Fortune family requests
your presence at the weddings of*

the Grooms

*Silhouette Desire's provocative new miniseries
featuring the beloved Fortune family and
five of your favorite authors.*

Bride of Fortune–August 2000
by Leanne Banks (SD #1311)

Mail-Order Cinderella–September 2000
by Kathryn Jensen (SD #1318)

Fortune's Secret Child–October 2000
by Shawna Delacorte (SD #1324)

Husband–or Enemy?–November 2000
by Caroline Cross (SD #1330)

Groom of Fortune–December 2000
by Peggy Moreland (SD #1336)

*Don't miss these unforgettable romances . . .
available at your favorite retail outlet.*

Silhouette®
Where love comes alive™

Visit Silhouette at www.eHarlequin.com

SDFCTG

Silhouette®

where love comes alive—online...

Visit the *Author's Alcove*

➢ Find the most complete information anywhere on your favorite Silhouette author.

➢ Try your hand in the Writing Round Robin— contribute a chapter to an online book in the making.

Enter the *Reading Room*

➢ Experience an interactive novel—help determine the fate of a story being created now by one of your favorite authors.

➢ Join one of our reading groups and discuss your favorite book.

Drop into *Shop eHarlequin*

➢ Find the latest releases—read an excerpt or write a review for this month's Silhouette top sellers.

➢ Try out our amazing search feature—tell us your favorite theme, setting or time period and we'll find a book that's perfect for you.

All this and more available at

www.eHarlequin.com
on Women.com Networks

SEYRB1

**Don't miss
an exciting opportunity
to save on the purchase of
Harlequin and Silhouette books!**

Buy any two Harlequin or
Silhouette books and save
$10.00 off future Harlequin
and Silhouette purchases

OR

buy any three
Harlequin or Silhouette books
and save **$20.00 off** future
Harlequin and Silhouette purchases.

*Watch for details
coming in October 2000!*

PHQ400

If you enjoyed what you just read,
then we've got an offer you can't resist!

Take 2 bestselling love stories FREE!
Plus get a FREE surprise gift!

Clip this page and mail it to Silhouette Reader Service™

IN U.S.A.	IN CANADA
3010 Walden Ave.	P.O. Box 609
P.O. Box 1867	Fort Erie, Ontario
Buffalo, N.Y. 14240-1867	L2A 5X3

YES! Please send me 2 free Silhouette Desire® novels and my free surprise gift. Then send me 6 brand-new novels every month, which I will receive months before they're available in stores. In the U.S.A., bill me at the bargain price of $3.34 plus 25¢ delivery per book and applicable sales tax, if any*. In Canada, bill me at the bargain price of $3.74 plus 25¢ delivery per book and applicable taxes**. That's the complete price and a savings of at least 10% off the cover prices—what a great deal! I understand that accepting the 2 free books and gift places me under no obligation ever to buy any books. I can always return a shipment and cancel at any time. Even if I never buy another book from Silhouette, the 2 free books and gift are mine to keep forever. So why not take us up on our invitation. You'll be glad you did!

225 SEN C222
326 SEN C223

Name	(PLEASE PRINT)	
Address	Apt.#	
City	State/Prov.	Zip/Postal Code

* Terms and prices subject to change without notice. Sales tax applicable in N.Y.
** Canadian residents will be charged applicable provincial taxes and GST.
   All orders subject to approval. Offer limited to one per household.
   ® are registered trademarks of Harlequin Enterprises Limited.

DES00   ©1998 Harlequin Enterprises Limited

COMING NEXT MONTH

#1321 THE DAKOTA MAN—Joan Hohl
Man of the Month
Mitch Grainger always got what he wanted…and what he wanted was his new assistant, Maggie Reynolds. The cunning businessman decided to make Maggie his reward in the ultimate game of seduction…never dreaming *his* heart might become *her* pawn.

#1322 RANCHER'S PROPOSITION—Anne Marie Winston
Body & Soul
All he wanted was a woman to share his ranch—not his bed. But when Lyn Hamill came to work on Cal McCall's South Dakota spread, he began to rethink his intentions. And though Lyn's eyes spoke of a dark past, Cal was determined to make her his wife in every way....

#1323 FIRST COMES LOVE—Elizabeth Bevarly
She'd had a crush on him since she was seven. But it wasn't until her entire hometown suspected Tess Monahan was pregnant that Will Darrow suddenly started showing up at her house offering a helping hand. Now if she could only convince him that she didn't want his hand but his heart....

#1324 FORTUNE'S SECRET CHILD—Shawna Delacorte
Fortune's Children: The Grooms
He thought he would never see Cynthia McCree again. Then suddenly she was back in town—and back in Shane Fortune's life. He had never stopped caring for the vulnerable beauty, but once he discovered the truth about her past, would he still want to make her his Fortune bride?

#1325 MAROONED WITH A MARINE—Maureen Child
Bachelor Battalion
One hurricane, one motel room—and one very sexy Marine—added up to trouble for Karen Beckett. She knew that Gunnery Sergeant Sam Paretti wouldn't leave her alone in the storm. But how did she convince him to stay once the danger had passed…?

#1326 BABY: MacALLISTER-MADE—Joan Elliott Pickart
The Baby Bet
They had one passionate night together, one that best friends Brenda Henderson and Richard MacAllister knew should never be repeated. Then Brenda announced she was pregnant. Now Richard had to convince Brenda that his proposal of marriage was not based on duty…but on love.

CMN0900